Fanfare

FOURTEEN STORIES ON A MUSICAL THEME

edited by
Duncan Minshull
and *Helen Wallace*

Published by BBC Worldwide Limited, Woodlands, 80 Wood Lane,
London W12 0TT

First published 1999
Selection and introduction copyright © Duncan Minshull and Helen Wallace 1999
Stories © individual copyright holders
These stories first appeared in BBC Music Magazine and were transmitted
on BBC Radio 3 1993–9
The copyright notices on page 4 represent an extension of this copyright page

ISBN: 0 563 38471 9

Set in Garamond 3 by BBC Worldwide
Printed and bound by Redwood Books Limited, Trowbridge
Cover printed by Belmont Press Limited, Northampton

CONTENTS

∿

DUNCAN MINSHULL is Senior Producer, Readings, for Radio 3 and Radio 4. He is editor of *Telling Stories*, Vols. 1–4 and is currently working on the *Vintage Book of Walking*. He also reviews for various newspapers and magazines.

HELEN WALLACE is Deputy Editor, *BBC Music Magazine*. She edited *The Strad* magazine, *Classical Music America* and the *BBC Music Magazine Guide to Music Education*. She is also a music critic for *The Times*.

The publishers would like to thank the following for their permission to use copyright material.

Fantasia on a Favourite Waltz © William Boyd 1998.
All rights reserved, enquiries to The Agency (London) Ltd

New Music © Carol Shields 1998

La Fanfare © Christopher Hope 1998.
Reproduced by permission of the author
c/o Rogers Coleridge & White

The Irresistible Don © Advanpress Limited 1999

The Dancing-Master's Music © William Trevor 1996

Beehernz © Penelope Fitzgerald 1997

Shell Songs © Clare Boylan 1998.
Reproduced by permission of the author
c/o Rogers Coleridge & White

Concerto Grossman © Byronic Investments Ltd 1998.
Reproduced by permission of the author
c/o Rogers Coleridge & White

Like a Circle in a Spiral © Russell Hoban 1999

The Yellow-haired Boy © Michèle Roberts 1999

Theory and Practice © Candia McWilliam 1999

The Over-ride © Rose Tremain 1996

The Last Picnic © James Hamilton-Paterson 1995

Corporate Entertainment © Helen Simpson 1999

EDITORS' NOTE

The *Radio 3/Music Magazine* short story began in 1993, with the aim of giving our listeners and readers a regular shot of fiction. Frederic Raphael was the first contributor, thirteen others followed him, their stories being broadcast and published at the same time. As the series gathered momentum, it seemed only natural to collect them. And how best to describe the riches ahead? Our brief to the writers was simple: delve into the world of music – any world, any music – and find a narrative that grips.

By tradition, musicians have never been afraid to put pen to paper – be it journalism, memoirs, libretti, sometimes fiction. On the other hand, music is a rare inspiration for story-tellers. But when they do explore the medium, how can we expect them to *use* it? After all they are not experts, just listeners. Needless to say, the results intrigued us. Some had moved into the shoes of music-makers, artfully reconstructing a life or work. Others looked at music in a mythical or abstract way. In these worlds you will meet reclusive conductors, itinerant pianists and Celtic choristers. There is a ghost evoked by Sixties pop. There is a brass band on the brink of disaster.

Our collection hits the bookshops, aptly, on the eve of this year's Proms (a story by Sir John Mortimer marks the event). We think it reflects the cream of short story writers working today. And if you missed any of these gems first time round, or you simply wish to revisit them, then read on.

Duncan Minshull and *Helen Wallace,* May 1999

FANTASIA ON A FAVOURITE WALTZ

William Boyd

CLARA BILLROTH HANDED THE BABY to Frau Schäfer and the child went gladly to the old woman, its cries diminishing to gurgles and whimpers. 'Say goodbye to your Mama,' Frau Schäfer said uselessly, as she did each evening, taking the baby's wrist between finger and thumb and making the tiny fingers parody a farewell wave. 'Say "Goodbye Mama". Say it, Ulrich.' 'Please don't call him Ulrich,' Clara said, 'I don't like the name.' 'You've got to give him a name soon,' Frau Schäfer said, hurt, 'the child's nearly four months old. It's not correct. It's not Christian.' 'Oh, all right, I'll try and think of one,' Clara said and turned away, pulling her shawl around her as she went down the stairs, feeling the cold wind rush up from the tenement door to meet her. April, she thought: it still might as well be winter.

She walked briskly down Jägerstrasse towards St Pauli, a little late, her shoes pinching her feet, making her shorten her pace, making her favour the right foot over the left. The left was sore. Annelies said that your feet were never exactly the same size, you should have a different shoe made for each foot. Annelies and her nonsense. In what world would that be, Clara wondered? How rich would you have to be to have a different…

She saw the boy leaning against the gas lamp, holding on to it with both hands as if it were a mast and he were on the pitching deck of a ship in a stormy sea. As she drew nearer she watched him press his forehead to the cool moisture-beaded metal. The wind off the harbour was full of threatening rain and the gas lamps wore their mist-drop halos like shimmering crowns in the gathering dark. The boy, she saw, was about fourteen or fifteen with long hair – reddish blonde – folded on his collar. His eyes were shut and he seemed to be speaking silently to himself. 'Hey,' Clara said, watchfully, 'Are you all right?' He opened his eyes and turned to her. He was a stocky young fellow with good features, blue eyes, the thick honey blonde hair drawn off his forehead in a wave. 'Thank you,' the boy said, blinking his pale-lashed blue eyes at her. He had a distinct Hamburg accent. 'Migraine,' he said. 'You wouldn't believe the headache I have. But I'll be fine. I just have to wait until it's passed. You are kind to stop, but I'll be fine.' Clara peered at him: his eyes were shadowed with the effort of talking. Sometimes she had these headaches herself, especially after little Katherina had died and then when she was pregnant with the baby boy, whatever she would call him – with 'Ulrich'. 'All right then,' she said. 'But don't let the police see you. They'll think you're drunk.' The stocky boy laughed politely and Clara went on her footsore way.

CLARA ARRANGED THE FRONT OF HER DRESS so that her bosom bulged freely over the bodice. The men liked that, it always worked. She tugged the front lower, arching her back, contemplating her reflection in the glass, turning left and right. She looked pretty tonight, she thought: the cold wind off the Elbe had brought colour to her face. She dipped her finger in the pot of rouge and added a little more to each cheek and a dab on her lips. She wanted to make a good impression on her first night;

Herr Knipe would be pleased with her. She was early too, none of the other girls were there and when she came through the bar the glasses were being polished and the dance floor swept. It seemed a prosperous place, this *Lokal*, not like the last one, there were even sheets on the bed. Herr Knipe seemed more generous too – keep half, my dear, he had said, and the more you work the happier I am.

In the bar the pianist had arrived and was sitting on the little raised dais, playing notes again and again as if he was tuning the piano. She walked towards him to introduce herself – it was important to befriend the musicians, then they would play your favourite melodies. The pianist heard her footsteps crossing the dance floor and turned. 'Hey,' Clara said, surprised. 'Migraine-boy. What're you doing here?' He smiled. 'I work here,' he said. 'How's the head?' Clara asked. He had the clearest blue eyes, all shadow gone from them now. 'Bearable.' He was trying not to look at her bosom, she saw. 'What's your name?' she said. He was too young to be working here, fourteen or fifteen only. 'Ah, Hannes,' he said. 'Hannes... Kreisler.' 'I'm Clara, Clara Billroth. Do you know any waltzes?' 'Oh yes,' said the boy Hannes, 'I know any number of waltzes.' 'Do you know this one?' Clara sang a few notes. 'It's my favourite.' Hannes frowned: 'You are not a very good singer, I'm afraid,' he said. 'Is it like this?' He turned to the piano and with his right hand picked out the tune. 'Yes,' Clara said, singing along, and then she saw him bring his left hand up to the piano and suddenly the dance hall was filled with the waltz, her waltz, her favourite waltz. She was amazed, as she always was, how they could take a simple tune, a few notes, and within seconds they were playing away – with both hands, no sheet music – it was as if they had known the waltz all their lives. Clara swayed to and fro to the rhythms. 'You're quite good, young Kreisler, my lad. Oh my God, look there's Herr Knipe. I'd better go.'

∾

FOUR MEN – FORTY MARKS, twenty for her, a fair start. A fat sailor, then his little friend. Then some dances. Then a salesman from Altona who proudly showed her a daguerrotype of his wife – she hated it when they did that. Then a dark, muscly fellow – Norwegian or Swedish – who smelt of fish. Clara sniffed at her shoulder, worried that it had rubbed off on her. He had heaved and heaved, the Norseman, took his time. None of her tricks seemed to work. Took his own sweet time.

She finished her beer, pulled the sheets back up and tucked them in. She was unhooking her shawl when there was a knock at her door. It was Hannes. 'Hey, little Kreisler. Thank you for playing my waltz.' 'It's quite pretty, your waltz,' Hannes said, 'I like the tune.' 'Want some beer?' Clara said. 'No, I must go,' Hannes said, 'I came to say goodbye.' 'I'll see you tomorrow,' Clara said. She noticed he was looking at her bosom again. 'No, no, I'm going away,' he said. 'To convalesce. I'm not very well.' He smiled at her wearily, 'I can't take any more of these migraines. I think my head will explode.' Clara shrugged, 'Well, I hope they get someone as good as you on the piano.' They walked down the stairs to the rear entrance together. 'That was real class tonight, Hannes, my boy. You're a talent, you know.' Hannes chuckled politely, the sort of polite chuckle, Clara thought, that told her he knew full well just how talented he was. They paused at the door, Clara tying her shawl in a knot, pulling it over her head. 'So, hello and goodbye, Hannes Kreisler.' Then she kissed him, as a sort of goodbye present really, and because he had been nice to her, one of her full kisses, with her tongue deep in his mouth, to give him something to remember her by, and she let him fumble and squeeze for a while at her breasts before she pushed him away with a laugh, clapped him on the shoulder and said, 'That's enough for you, my young fellow, I'm off to my bed.'

∞

IT WAS FUNNY HOW EVERYTHING could change in a year, Clara thought, as she wandered through Alster Arcade looking at the fine stores. She liked to do this before she went down to St Pauli for her evening's work. '47 had been, well, not too bad, but '48?... My God, not so good. If only Herr Knipe hadn't died. If only Frau Schäfer hadn't gone to live with her son in Hildesheim, if only the baby had been healthier, not so many doctors needed. Money. All she thought about was money. And everywhere there was revolution, they said, and all she could think about was money. She looked at her reflection in the plate glass window of Vogts & Co. She should put a bit more weight back on: the gentlemen didn't like skinny girls these days. She sighed and went to stand in a patch of sunlight 'to warm my tired old bones,' she told herself, with a chuckle, 'for a moment or two.'

There was a big piano store across the street, the pianos in the window lustrous and glossy, their lids up, the grained wood agleam with wax polish. The early summer warmth meant that the double doors of the shop were thrown open and she could hear over the noise of the cabs and the horse trams the demonstrator inside playing away at the waltz. Dum dee dee, dum dee dee... Good God in Heaven, she thought, that's my waltz.

It was little Hannes Kreisler all right, Clara saw, though not so little any more, the back was broader, the jaw squarer, the hair longer, if anything, playing away on the small stage in the centre of the great emporium, but he wasn't calling himself

Hannes Kreisler, these days. The fancy copperplate on the placard that advertised the demonstrator's name (and his address for piano lessons) read 'Karl Wurth'.

Clara strolled into the shop, grateful that it was busy, thinking that with a bit of luck no one would tell her to leave for a while. A small crowd stood in a semicircle around 'Karl Wurth' listening to him play. It was her waltz, that was true, but it was different also, the tune was freer: it kept changing, changing pace and rhythm and then coming back to the original notes. She edged closer, watching Hannes play, seeing that he was reading music, there were sheets propped in front of him, concentrating, staring at the notes. The music grew faster and then finished in a kind of a gallop and a series of shuddering chords, not like a waltz at all. He slowly took his hands away from the keyboard. There was applause and Hannes looked round with his fleeting smile and gave a small dipping bow before he stood up and stepped away from the piano, taking his sheet music and removing the placard with his new name.

'Well, hey, if it isn't the famous pianist Herr Karl Wurth,' Clara said, tugging at his coat tail. He turned and recognised her at once, she saw, and that pleased her. 'Clara,' he said, 'What a surprise.' 'How's the nut?' Clara said, reaching up and tapping his forehead. 'How's the brain-ache?' 'Much better,' Hannes said. 'I spent last summer at Winsen. Perfect. Full recovery. Do you know it?' 'Winsen? Oh I'm never away from the place,' Clara said. 'That was my waltz you were playing. You've even written it down.' He had rolled his sheet music up into a tight baton. 'Here,' he said, handing it to her. 'It's a present.' 'How will you play it, if you give it to me?' she said. 'Oh, it needs improving. I'll do some more work. It's all up here,' he tapped his head. 'So Clara, still at Knipe's *Lokal*? he asked. 'He's dead,'

Clara said, 'Tuberculosis. It all changed. I've moved – to a place on Kastanienallee. They could do with a decent pianist, I can tell you. So if you're looking for a position, I'll put in a good word.'

Hannes was about to speak but another boy appeared beside him carrying a music case. 'And who might this charming young lady be?' the boy said. He had lively, mobile features, dark hair and a pointed chin. 'This is Clara,' Hannes said. 'An old friend. And this is my brother Fritz. Who's late.' 'My apologies,' Fritz said, and bowed to Clara. 'He – that one –' pointing at Hannes, 'is a slave driver,' he said and stepped up on to the stage and opened his case taking out sheets of music. 'I have to leave,' Hannes said. 'I have a piano lesson to give.' 'We all have to earn a living,' Clara said. 'On you go. I'll look at the pianos.' They shook hands. 'What's become of your *Lokal?*' Hannes said, lowering his voice. 'Maybe I'll pass by.' She wanted to tell him but she decided not to. 'Oh no, it's not the place for you, Hannes Kreisler Karl Wurth.' 'I'll find it,' he said. 'Kastanienallee isn't so big. I probably worked in it. I worked in a lot of these places.' So she told him the name: Flugel's. What was wrong with that, she argued, he was almost a man, he was earning some money, why should she turn away the chance of earning some money herself? 'Please take this,' he said, handing her his scroll of sheet music again. 'A souvenir.' She took it from him. 'See you soon, Clara,' he said, but they both knew that was very unlikely; still, you never could tell about a man and his appetites. 'For sure,' she said, 'Come by any time after six. We'll have a dance.'

She managed to look at the pianos for a few minutes before one of the floor managers asked her to leave. As she walked past the demonstrator's stage Fritz Wurth smiled at her and nodded goodbye. Except his name wasn't Fritz Wurth at all, she now

13

saw as she glanced at his placard, it was Fritz Brahms. Brahms. What were they like, these boys? First Kreisler, then Wurth, now Brahms – it was all a game to them.

∞

SHE RODE IN THE OMNIBUS down to St Pauli trying not to think of the floor manager's expression as he had asked her to leave. To distract herself she unrolled the sheet music Hannes had given her. Hannes had been kind, decent, he had remembered her. All written by hand, too, the little squiggly black scratching of the notes. How can they play from that? His brother had been polite also. She read the title slowly, her lips moving as she formed the words: *Fantasia on a Favourite Waltz*. A souvenir. A nice gesture. She said it out loud, softly: *Phantasie über einen beliebten Walzer*... There were some decent people about in the world, not many, but a few of them. Hannes. It was a good name, that: maybe that was what she should call the baby. Hannes Billroth. She was still musing on the baby's new name when she arrived at Herr Flugel's *Lokal*. Hannes Billroth – it had a ring to it. It was only when she took her position by the bar, and the pianist started thundering away noisily at a boring old polka that she realised she had left the music behind her in the horse tram. It made her angry at her carelessness, for a moment or two, before she asked herself what she could possibly do with such a manuscript anyway, and certainly that ape pounding away on the piano wouldn't have been able to make head nor tail of it, not something so delicate and beautiful. *Phantasie über einen beliebten Walzer*. I ask you. Head nor tail.

∞

NEW MUSIC

Carol Shields

SHE WAS TWENTY-ONE WHEN HE FIRST SAW HER, seated rather primly next to him on the Piccadilly Line, heading toward South Kensington. It was mid-afternoon. Like every other young woman in London, she was dressed from head to toe in a depthless black, and on her lap sat a leather satchel.

It was the sort of satchel a girl might inherit from her adoring barrister father, and this was the truth of the matter (he found out later), except that the father was a piano teacher, not a barrister, and that his adoration was often shaded by exasperation – which one can understand.

After a moment of staring straight ahead, she snapped open her satchel, withdrawing several sheets of paper covered with musical notations. (*He* was on his way to Imperial College for a lecture on reinforced concrete; *she* was about to attend an advanced class in Baroque music.) He had never before seen anyone 'read' music in quite this way, silently, as though it were a newspaper, her eyes running back and forth, left to right, top of the page to the bottom, then flipping to the next. The notes looked cramped and fussy and insistent, but she took in every one, blinking only when she shifted to a new page. He imagined that her head was filled with a swirl of musical lint, that she was actually 'hearing' a tiny concert inside that casually combed head of hers. And *his* head? – it was crammed with different

stuff: equations, observations, a set of graphs, the various gradi-
ents of sands and gravels, his upcoming examinations, and the
fact that his trousers pocket had a hole in it, leaking a shower of
coins on to the floor as he stood up.

'I think this is yours,' she said, handing him a dropped
penny.

'Whose music is that?' he managed. 'The music you're
looking at?'

'Tallis. Thomas Tallis.'

'Oh.'

She took pity on him as they stepped together on to the
platform. 'Sixteenth-century. English.'

'Is he?' – inane question – 'is he good?'

'Good?'

'His music? – is it, you know, wonderful? Is he a genius,
would you say?'

She stopped and considered. They were in the street now.
The sunshine was sharply aslant. 'He was the most gifted
composer of his time,' she recited, 'until the advent of William
Byrd.'

'You mean this Byrd person came along and he was better
than Thomas What's-his-name?'

'Oh' – she looked affronted – 'I don't think better is quite the
word. William Byrd was more inventive than Thomas Tallis,
that's all. More original, in my opinion anyway.'

'Then why' – this seemed something he had to know, even
though his reasoning was sure to strike her as simplistic and
stupid – 'why are you carrying around Thomas Tallis's music
instead of the other chap's – the one who was better?'

She stared at him. Then she smiled and shrugged. 'Do you
always insist on the very best?'

'I don't know,' he said, not being someone who'd experienced much in the way of choices. He was conscious of his hideous ignorance and inability to express himself. 'It just seems like a waste of time. You know, taking second best when you could have the best.'

'Like reading, hmmm, Marlowe when you could have Shakespeare?'

He nodded, or at least attempted to nod.

'It's *because* I believe Tallis is second best that I prefer him,' she told him then. Her chin went up. Her voice was firm. 'I don't expect you to understand.'

'I do, I do,' he exclaimed in his awful voice. And it was true, he did.

He loved her. Right from that instant, the way she opened up her mouth and said *because Tallis is second best*.

∾

IMAGINE A WOMAN GETTING OUT OF BED one hour earlier than the rest of the household. What will she do with that hour?

Make breakfast scones for her husband and three school-age children? Not this woman, not scones, banish the thought. Will she press her suit skirt? clean out her handbag? ready her attaché case for a day at work? No, this woman works at home – at a computer set up in what was once, in another era, in another incarnation, a sewing room. It's a room with discoloured wallpaper, irises climbing on a sort of trellis, which doesn't make sense for a non-climbing, earthbound flower, Against one wall is her writing table, which is really a cheap plywood door laid flat on trestles. She has been offered, several times, a proper desk, but she actually prefers this makeshift affair – which wobbles slightly each time she puts her elbow on the table and stares into the screen.

That's where she is now. At this hour! Her old and not-very-clean mauve dressing gown is pulled tight against the chill. It is not a particularly flattering colour, but she doesn't know this, and besides, she's as faithful to old clothes as she is to inferior wallpaper. It's as though she can't bear to hurt their feelings. She's tapping away, without so much as a cup of coffee to cheer her on. It's still dark outside, not black exactly but a brew of streaked grey. You'd think she'd put up a curtain or at least a blind to soften that staring grey rectangle, but no. Nor has she thought to turn on the radio for a little musical companionship, she of all people. She's tapping, tapping at her keyboard, her two index fingers taking turns, and for the moment that's all she appears to need.

Is she writing a letter to her mother in Yorkshire? A Letter to the Editor complaining about access ramps for the handicapped? A suicide note full of blame and forgiveness and deliberate little shafts of self-pity? No. Today she's writing the concluding page (page 612) of a book, a book she's been working on for four years now, the comprehensive biography of Renaissance composer Thomas Tallis, c1505–1585. The penultimate paragraph is already on the screen, then the concluding paragraph itself, and now, as a scarf of soft light flows in through the window and lands on her shoulders, she taps in the last sentence, and then the final word – which is the burnished, heightened, blurted-out word: 'triumph'. The full sentence reads: 'Nevertheless Tallis's contribution to English music can be described as a triumph.'

Nevertheless? What's all this *nevertheless* about, you're probably asking?

Squinting into the screen, she taps in 'The End', but immediately deletes it. My guess is that she's decided writing 'The

End' is too self-conscious a gesture. Did her husband write 'The End' when he finished his monograph *Distribution of Gravel Resources in Southwest England*? Yes, certainly, but then he's not as fearful of self-indulgence as she.

She's spent four years on this book. I've already said that, haven't I? – but to be fair, the first eight months were passed listening to Tallis's music itself. The Mass for Four Voices, *Spem in alium, Lamentations of Jeremiah*, nine motets, and so on. She lay on our canted, worn sofa – the kids at school, the husband at the office – and listened with note pad and pencil on her sweatered chest, waiting for the magnetic atoms of musical matter to come together, one and one and one, and give shape to the man who created them. There's so little known about him, and what is known is made blurry with *might have, could have, possibly was* – all the maddening italics of a rigorously undocumented life. The only real resource is the music, which, curiously, has come down to our century intact, or so I'm told, and that is why this woman spent eight months absorbing each separate, self-contained, cellular note.

Occasionally she fell asleep during those long sofa days. I'm no expert, but I've been told that Tallis is not particularly interested in counterpoint as such, and that the straightforward way he develops his musical ideas produces a sense of serenity which can be an invitation to doze. She admits this, but insists he can be experimental when he wants to be and even mildly extravagant. (An *In nomine* she gives as an example.)

∞

TALLIS'S GHOST LIVES IN OUR HOUSE, his flat, hummy, holy tones and the rise and fall of Latin phrasing; it's permeated the carpets and plaster; it clings to the family hair and clothing and gets into the food. And for several months now an inky photocopy of his portrait has been stuck on the fridge, a little wraith of a man with a small pointed beard and abundant shoulder-length hair brushed back from his forehead. He is vain about his hair, one can tell.

It's not easy to calculate overall height from a head-and-shoulder image, but clearly he's got the alarmed, doubting eyes of a short man. (I am not a particularly tall chap myself, and so I instantly recognise and connect with a short man's uneasy gaze.) The children are forever asking their mother how Tom Tallis is getting along, meaning is she going to finish her book soon. They miss her rhubarb crumble, they miss the feel of ironed clothes and clean sheets and socks sorted into pairs. Her husband — he's in the sand and gravel business — he misses waking up beside her in the morning. By the time the alarm goes at half-seven, the bed is cold, and she's already been working for an hour or more at her secondhand word processor. 'There's cornflakes,' she calls out when she hears footsteps in the kitchen, not for a moment lifting her eyes from the screen. 'There's plenty of bread for toast.' Well, sometimes there is and sometimes there isn't.

But because this is the final morning in the writing of her book, with the book's closing word 'triumph' winking at her from the screen, she rises and stretches and makes her way to the kitchen, a sleepy, mauve-toned phantom. There she finds them — two sons, daughter and spouse, gathered about the toaster. She stares as though we are strangers who have entered her house sometime during the last four years and are now engaged in a mystical rite around this small smudged appliance. We're not exactly unwelcome, her look tells us, but the nature of our presence has yet to be explained.

Two months later Thomas Tallis is still on the fridge door.

No one in the family has quite the courage to take him down, but the manuscript, all 612 pages, has been mailed to the publisher. This is a reasonably distinguished publishing house – though certainly not the best – and the editor is delighted to have the Tallis book on his autumn list. He would much rather the author had written about William Byrd, of course, that goes without saying. There would have been *great* interest in a book about William Byrd, whereas there is only *considerable* interest in Thomas Tallis. Tallis, if the truth be known, must always be identified along with his famous student who, according to tradition, overshadowed him. Part of Tallis's essence, in fact, is that he is stuck in an inevitable frame of reference. He also ran. Ran a good race but…

∞

IMAGINE WHAT A WOMAN DOES who has suddenly, after four long years, completed an arduous task. She cleans her house, for one thing, not perfectly, but competently. She remains in bed an hour longer in the morning, and for this her husband is ecstatically grateful. They wake together, his lips trace the pearled curve of her spinal column. He is a man who stumbles about all day dealing with the exigencies of gravel production, gravel deliveries, gravel prices per cubic metre, but thinking every other minute of his wife's soft limbs, her bodily clefts and swellings.

For her clever daughter she buys tickets to the ballet, and they return from the performance drunk with pleasure, and enact mock, foolish pirouettes on the hall carpet, bumping into the walls and giggling like a pair of teenagers.

For her younger son, a boy of exceptional beauty, she spends a whole day sorting through the debris of his bedroom. She does this tactfully, tidily, thoroughly, and the child is conscious of an immense sense of relief. All those buried socks, books, pencil ends, wads of paper, coins, dust – he was unable to deal with it, but now all is order and ease.

Her middle child is neither clever nor exceptional in appearance, but she loves him best; she can't help it; he touches a spot of tenderness in her that only music has been able to reach. She kisses the top of his head while he eats his cereal. She straightens the collar of his coat before he leaves for school. She has gone back to listening to Tallis in the afternoons, a remarkable recording by the Tallis Scholars, and as she listens something like a kite string reaches down and pulls at her thoughts, which are not quite ready to be thoughts. It might be that she's putting her own heart beside itself, making comparisons. What does it mean to be better or best?

One of the new, young music gurus, writing in the weekend papers, believes Tallis is actually a better composer than Byrd. What had been considered simple in his work is now thought of as subtle. What struck earlier critics as primitive is really a form of understated sophistication. Perhaps these judgements boil down to mere fashion. Or perhaps the recent Tallis biography has upped his reputation.

∞

IMAGINE A GIRL JUST TWENTY-ONE YEARS OLD – I'm aware that I probably should say 'young woman', but there is so much girlishness in her face and in the way she sets off from home each morning, running a quarter of a mile to the Tube station, swinging her leather satchel at her side. She is probably in love or at least drawn to the possibility of love. Undoubtedly she thinks about the new clenched knot of ardour in her chest, thinks of it all day long, coming and going to her classes, while seated at the piano and also at the harpsichord, which she has recently taken up. Her head may be swarming with Latin, with choral efforts, with the rising and falling and patterning of sound, but her body presses against this new, rapturous apparition.

Then one day, late in May, she meets a young man. They collide on the Tube, not the most romantic of venues. This man is awkward, he has holes in his pockets, he is ungainly in his appearance. He is really rather ordinary, as a matter of fact, immersed as he is in the drainage capability of compacted gravel, and so lacking in perception that he will never under- 25 stand why she agreed to have a coffee with him instead of attending her class. He's a lad, that's all, just another face, though he flatters himself that she sees something in him. Why, otherwise, does she go to the cinema with him on that first afternoon, and then out for fish and chips, and later, only a week later, does she end up in his flat, in his bed?

Why does she marry him, him of all people? Why do they buy a house in a semi-respectable area of London, produce three quite nice children, take holidays in Scotland or else in Yorkshire where her mother lives? And why – another question altogether – when her book on Tallis is launched at a large cocktail buffet, and her publisher suggests that she write about William Byrd, does she shake her head, 'no'?

Let someone else do Byrd, her looks said on that occasion.

But now, one year later, she's rethinking the matter. Yes, Byrd. Why not?

The system of temperament in the family shifts once again, and so does the onward allotment of time. As before, this woman rises early each day, but this time to put together her notes on William Byrd, the divine William Byrd, who seems suddenly in danger of being eclipsed by his renowned teacher and mentor.

She allows the house to fill up with dust and clutter. When her husband drops a kiss on the back of her neck, she shakes her hair impatiently. Her word processor sends out blinding windows of authority. She's busy, she's preoccupied, she's committing an act of redemption. A choir of ten thousand voices sings inside her head. No wonder she's been looking at her husband lately with an odd, assessing, measuring clarity.

More and more he tries to stay out of her way, and more and more he refers to himself in the third person. He's an ordinary man, no one to make a fuss over. He insists on that.

Nevertheless he finds himself opening his ears to the new music that's overtaken the house.

LA FANFARE

Christopher Hope

THIERRY AND I WERE SITTING on red plush banquettes in the Café du Commerce. Whenever the door opened, the room shivered. It was February and the wind had snow on its breath.

Thierry had badgered me to drive him over the mountains to see the carnival in Limoux. Because he's so poor, Thierry hitches rides. A solitary trudger between villages, black leather shoes: a little man in a grey suit and a belted mac, lifting a thumb on the road between Narbonne and nowhere, sweating gently, carrying a briefcase. He looked like a debt collector, or a professional mourner – why should anyone stop?

Edith stopped. She had given him a lift in her mauve Twingo.

Thierry told her he loved music. He meant Mozart.

Edith said she loved music. She meant marching bands. Come to the Café du Commerce, she said.

And there we sat. Bright and clean, shining glasses and waiters who tried to ignore Thierry. Full of men in funny hats, puffing into tubas and clarinets. In one corner a flute player. And lined up at the bar, drinking pastis, four saxophonists and a triangle player.

They were the band, the *fanfare*, who marched round the town square, ahead of their float, every night during Carnival, from January to March.

They have names – The Arcades, and The Miller's Men.

That night belonged to The Blanquetiéres. They make the sparkling white wine of Limoux. They wore red neckerchiefs and pointy black hats and laughed a lot. It was a carnival joke. Hicks, and proud of it! Bumpkins dressed as yokels. Let's face it, this band was not the Vienna Philharmonic. And they played things like 'My Father's Moustache' and 'The Devil in a Dustbin' and 'O, dear Ramona!'. They were young, they laughed a lot.

They weren't Thierry's kind of people. He's from Paris and he suffers terribly in the Midi. There is a kind of rough gaiety he can't manage.

They were having fun. Solid blokes. When they weren't being the *fanfare*, they were in the rugby team. The room was full of that braying, demented sound of a band tuning up; the boys shook spit from their mouthpieces; they blew into their instruments and scraps of tuba, trumpet, sax, flew past our ears like birds trapped in a room.

He watched them knocking back pastis and grew even paler. 'Wet lips, warm fingers.'

Thierry, aspirin pale, thin, starving, stroked his bald dome. He rubbed the faint white powdery stubble on his round chin. He called the waiter over and the waiter came, shielding his face as if Thierry gave off rays. It was as if his crumbling white shirt, black tie and big black eyes in his pale face said – he's bad news; an ex-con, a crazy.

He's not crazy but he is very strange. For one thing he's most curiously loud. He shakes the hands with a crushing grip and he booms away; in such a sunken chest, it is terrifyingly hearty, but you don't believe in it for a moment.

'Whisky,' Thierry told the waiter.

Languedoc is afloat in wine but he never touched what he called 'little wines', he drank only the 'big reds' of Bordeaux. He never compromised, never lowered his standards, did Thierry. He never paid either.

'I'll go to my grave like Dante.' Said Thierry.

He wouldn't. He would go in someone else's hearse, on someone else's money...

Thierry pulled at his scotch and said normally he drank only malted ten-year-old – and you had to admire him – because normally he drank water.   31

Then the carnival creatures began pushing through the glass doors. Two apache dancers in striped shirts, a burglar in a mask with a bag of swag, two Keystone Cops, a hunchback, a baby, several clowns with green hair and a couple of dwarfs, kids probably, in those blank white Venetian masks that look like walls with eyes.

In walked a fat little washerwoman with grey hair and cherry cheeks and blue laundry bag slung over her shoulder. When she lifted her mask, she was young and dark with lovely brown eyes. It was Edith. She wore blue jeans, and the general slackness of modern life. Until our sloppy times, Thierry believed, artists dressed with care – they wore their clothes with elegance. Even the rebels, say Baudelaire, and Rimbaud, even they looked like something.

Edith didn't say much. Just 'Bonjour Monsieur' and 'Ça va?' to Thierry, and went back to the gorilla.

∞

I HADN'T NOTICED THE GORILLA till then. He stood some way behind Edith, tapping a plastic orange truncheon in his palm.

Thierry smiled after her.

So now, mark me well, we have a man in a burgundy bow tie

grinning like an idiot at a girl dressed up as Widow Twankey. This man hates pantomime. This man detests the café, and the square beyond where roasted almonds are being hawked and balloons and crêpes and very sticky gaufrettes.

And Thierry loves only great women, usually dead women – and the washerwoman isn't Juliet. She isn't Madame de Pompadour or Cleopatra, or one of the great heroines of music or literature or even pornography. Thierry is no prude, he's happy with real greatness, wherever it is found – but she isn't Madame O either.

She's Edith from the Wine Co-op and she makes plonk.

But he thinks she's wonderful. A man who never tries small wines, only the great wines from Bordeaux. It's the big reds or nothing. Even sex is hard – it has its big reds.

'I'm not having as much as the Marquis de Sade,' he said when I asked him about it once.

Now the boys in the *fanfare* swallow their drinks and everyone goes outside into the bitter night. The carnival creatures gather behind their float; it is a steam engine, walked like a pantomime horse, by the two cops, drawn by a couple of clowns and accompanied, on either side, by the washerwoman and the gorilla.

The *fanfare* blares into life, blowing on to their fingers. The marchers start their strange, slow, snaking, stomping hand-waving dance, tracing the fingers left and right. There is something delicate about the waving fingers. It's Indian or Balinese. But it's local. Babies do it, you're born with it, in Limoux.

And Thierry taps his feet. 'What do you think?'

I say, 'Fine, I think she's fine.'

But what I am really thinking is why do the waiters shy away from Thierry? Do they have some sixth sense, like some animals sniff fire or danger?

That's when he said he was going to join the marchers.

I said he shouldn't. You don't join the marchers in Limoux, it's a private event. Outsiders can watch – no more than that. The locals don't want it. They haven't got themselves to this state of perfection, only to have strangers muscling in.

Thierry gave that thin frosty smile that says he's gone deaf and went outside into the freezing square.

33

I didn't see him for a while because it's traditional that the *fanfare* stops at each watering hole, and has a couple for the road. The progress around the arcades of the square takes about an hour.

But when they pulled up outside the Café du Commerce, I picked Thierry out. He was wearing a mask, the old man with the big nose and the black brows. He was horribly out of place. He's about as tall as Toulouse-Lautrec and he couldn't do the stamping voodoo dance, or the hand movements. He didn't have the hands, the rhythm.

It was a relief when the procession broke up and headed inside to the bar.

Thierry sat down, very pleased. I stared at the ceiling.

Edith came over. She pulled off her mask, dropped her bundle of washing on the floor and brushed her brown hair out of her eyes; a waiter brought her hot chocolate.

'You should not join,' Edith frowned and blew into her big cup.

Thierry smiled his deaf smile. 'I can do it. I did it.'

'You didn't. You can't,' said Edith.

The gorilla walked into the café then.

Thierry noticed nothing. He started talking about the

fanfare. He said it harked back to very early Europe, it was magic, it sang of rain, war, worship.

Edith was watching the gorilla, who had taken off his head and tucked it under his arm, like a crash helmet.

I was still trying to work out why Thierry had this dampening effect, why he rained on everyone's parade, when he marched – the other marchers lost rhythm, faltered – the tuba and the sax and the big bass drum all went to pieces. Thierry was like an inert gas, or an invasion force: get a dose of him in your system and everything grinds to a halt.

While I was mulling this over, the gorilla stepped up and hit Thierry several times on the head with his orange truncheon.

'You don't belong here,' the gorilla told Thierry.

And then he turned to Edith. 'Why do you go on meeting men on the quiet?'

Edith threw her hot chocolate at him then, and if he hadn't lifted his head to his face he might have been rather badly burnt.

No one else paid any attention. That's Carnival for you.

And then the musicians swallowed their drinks and went stumbling into the cold for another circuit of the square, and the gorilla and the washerwoman went with them. And it was quiet again. Thierry sat down. And I had the feeling he was replaying the hollow smack of the plastic truncheon on his small bald head.

And what does Thierry do about this? I'll tell you. He went into Carcassonne and got hold of Sven, a tall Swede, who keeps a boat on the Canal du Midi. Next he had a word with Sam the Englishman, who has a boat at Capstang. Then he got Monsieur Blondin, the carpenter, to use some of the spare wood – kept for making coffins – to build a couple of platforms, like flat wooden spoons.

Then Thierry went to talk to Jo-Jo, who runs a *fanfare* called The Hungry Uncle. Jo-Jo dresses like the late President Mitterrand in red scarf and dark blue overcoat. Thierry wanted The Uncle to play at dawn beside the Canal du Midi. Jo-Jo said no. The Hungry Uncle is a famous *fanfare*; they have made a CD.

Thierry didn't give up.

∾

THERE IS A *fanfare*, a poor, pockmarked band, which can be seen when the Cavalcade marches. The Cavalcade is a squadron of drum-majorettes; male majorettes, dumpy men in short, pleated tennis dresses, wigs and lipstick, glasses and beards, and they march behind La Tante Gallopante – The Galloping Auntie.

We're not talking about much. Just a tuba, two trumpets, four saxes, and a small boy who plays the drum which is attached to a clever wheel so he can push it ahead of him like a baby carriage. The Auntie dresses in red shirts and baggy black pants and they're a scrawny lot. Yves, the tuba player, is blind and he is led by his wife, a striking blonde.

Blind Yves married the best-looking woman for miles, and never clapped eyes on her. René, the bandleader, walks back- wards, counting time because The Galloping Auntie can't keep in step otherwise.

And René agreed to do it for nothing. The Galloping Auntie would be on the humpbacked bridge over the Canal du Midi, outside La Redort, at dawn on Sunday morning.

Thierry phoned the gorilla from the public phone box, on the road to Narbonne.

A challenge like that cannot go unanswered. In real life the gorilla was Luis, the eighth man in the Limoux rugby scrum.

As the mist was lifting off the canal that Sunday morning, Edith turned up in her Twingo. Luis was driving, naturally. This wasn't supposed to take long. Out of his gorilla suits, Luis looked like every other rugby player around here – dark and short with big neck muscles.

Thierry and Luis boarded their boats, and stepped on to the wooden platform the coffin-maker had fashioned. They were armed with long wooden lances. These were the rules: three passes, as the boats trundled towards each other, winner knocks his man into the water.

It is an ancient custom around here. A tournament on water. But usually it is elegant stuff, with great big boats and teams of rowers, and two fighters poised, lances high above the water. And a *fanfare* over in the stands. Like a bullfight afloat.

What we had, instead, were two tatty canal boats, with Sven the Swede saying, 'For god's sake don't fall anywhere near my propellers!' And Sam the Englishman saying, 'Keep your pecker up!' to Thierry who speaks no English, and wouldn't know a pecker if it bit him, and has never known which way is 'up', and squinting down his lance because his eyes are bad, while The Galloping Auntie stood miserably on the humpbacked bridge over the canal – groaning away.

And Edith, saying bitterly, 'I suppose I'm the prize?'

Then she locked herself into her mauve Twingo and began doing her nails and took care to look the other way as the two boats went chugging toward each other

Three times Luis knocked Thierry into the water. He had weeds in his hair and his underpants showed through his wet grey flannels. Sven hauled him out with the boat-hook and all the time The Galloping Auntie blared away on the bridge.

Three times was the deal. But Thierry spat water and said he'd go on. And so Luis knocked him off his perch again and again, and the *fanfare* wailed.

Four, five, six falls later, Sam stopped him.

'You'll drown, you fool.'

'Yes,' said Thierry, 'I will.'

Blind Yves's wife put a stop to it. She led her husband away because she could not bear to let him watch a man kill himself. So the *fanfare* packed it in, and you can't have a water tourna-ment without music.

And not once did Edith look at Thierry. He had made things impossible for her. Even if she hated Luis, she was saddled with him now.

∾

ON THE LAST NIGHT of the carnival, Thierry and I were back in Limoux. We were upstairs, in the Grand Café. The restaurant looks on to the square and you can see but not be seen. All the teams were marching. The square was packed. The last night is sacred; they bring out a man made of sticks and straw and fine clothes. They talk of him with great respect; he is 'Our Lord Carnival' and then they light a fire under him.

Thierry was very quiet. Sam the Englishman got it half right. If The Galloping Auntie had not packed up, and gone home, he would have drowned. He wasn't trying to kill himself. But he would have gone on till Luis killed him – or gave up.

All Thierry could say to me was, 'If someone wins, someone must go down.'

There was a finesse about that.

Thierry got there – the sharp edge – by using his head. The same head that the gorilla had hit him on. He played for keeps.

And that made him deadly. The others couldn't do that. For them, Carnival is a game and the *fanfare* is a bunch of rugby players in smocks, and it's all fun.

Thierry thought fun was lies. This was about living and luck and magic and hope. Life and the end of a life. Blood in the sand; death or glory; do or die, that's what the music of the *fanfare* said.

In the middle of the square the Lord of the Carnival was burning – his nose caught fire and then his straw hair. He danced in his burning wooden shoes like a hanged man and the *fanfares* wailed in anguished joy. And the gorilla waved his orange truncheon.

The waiter came over, shuffling sideways, not looking at Thierry.

I took the wine list; I found a very pricey Bordeaux, and I ordered a big red. But even as the man went off I wondered – Was it big enough? That was the problem. With Thierry. With love, with death.

∾

THE
IRRESISTIBLE
DON

John Mortimer

∾∾∾

'HERE IT COMES,' he said. 'The spirit of the irresistible Don.'

'It's exciting,' she said.

'Of course it's exciting.' He spoke, as ever, as though she were a continual source of amusement. 'And more exciting still from the front row of the box, after a glass of the company champagne. There's a good deal to be said for corporate entertaining.'

'But why *me?*' she asked him. 'You can't be expecting to sell *me* anything.'

'Don't you be too sure of that.' He might have added another sentence, but his voice was drowned in the breaking wave of applause as the distant, puppet-like figure of the conductor emerged from a door, shook hands with the orchestra leader and seemed to bounce, as though on strings, on to the podium and bow. He lifted his baton, bows were raised and hovered over strings, wind instruments approached pursed lips and Selina Wagstaff, small, blonde, twenty-five years old, felt the fingers of her right hand being interlocked with those on the left hand of Jason Tench, managing director of Clarion Television.

Jason was a quarter of a century older than the girl at his side, and had, and probably would have until his dying day, a look of boyish charm, a small grin which could be daring or vulnerable at will, wrinkles of laughter at the corners of his eyes and jet black hair, which looked as though it had been disturbed by a high wind or a restless night and was only very slightly flecked with grey. These assets had an effect on the female workers in Clarion TV and the multitude of his love affairs, both in and out of the office, were the subject of knowing laughter among the girls in reception and jealous amazement in the men's washroom. Selina had worked for him for almost two months. She had been surprised and vaguely disappointed to discover that, in spite of all the bad jokes and serious warnings of her friends in Clarion, Jason had behaved with the uninterested detachment of someone who had read, and was prepared to take seriously, the warnings in the company handbook against sexual harassment in the workplace. As she arranged meetings, and made coffee for potential advertisers, and as she daily encountered Jason's promising grin and unruly black hair she thought, occasionally, that a bit of sexual harassment might lighten up the day.

Not that Selina didn't have a boyfriend. She and Michael from 'human resources' had been going out, which usually meant staying in, together for almost two years, and they might have lived together if it weren't for an incompatibility. Michael was a Country and Western fan, whose idea of a musical evening was to go out in a checked shirt, jeans and, at his occasional worst, a Stetson hat, to the upper floor of a pub in Battersea to relive the great days of Dolly Parton. Selina's mother had been head of music in a local comprehensive and she had grown up to blasts of great symphonies and the soothing dialogue of string quartets. She couldn't have taken too many recordings of 'Stand By Your Man' and Mike had been known to fall asleep during any prolonged playing of the Brandenburg Concertos. So Jason's approach, being musical, was well calculated to win a prize that was half his already.

It happened when his car was being repaired and the garage rang to say it was ready for collection. Surprisingly he asked her to run him down to collect it and he folded his long legs in the front of her Renault 5 in the company car park. When she switched on the engine the tape took up where it had left off, in the middle of Mozart's Serenade for Thirteen Wind Instruments. She stretched out a hand to turn it off and he said, 'No, do leave it,' and after a short silence added, 'You must come with me to the box.'

'What box?' She had a moment of unreasoning fear that he was going to take her to watch two huge, half-naked men slugging each other's teeth out.

'Our box at the Proms.'

'I'd love to.'

He listened to the music for a while and then looked knowledgeable. 'That's Schubert, isn't it?' She didn't correct him and he gave her his infallible searching look. 'That's settled then.'

It was not entirely clear what was settled. For the next month he was, as usual, behaving exactly as the manual said he should. But then she found a programme of the Proms on her desk, open at the first concert, which was to contain a Mozart piano concerto and the *Jupiter* Symphony. When she noticed that the programme started with the overture to *Don Giovanni*, she allowed herself a small and secret smile. Even if he hadn't picked the programme for her deliberately, she had no doubt as to his ultimate intention. So her question, 'Why me?', was one to which she already knew the answer, and although his reply was drowned in the expectant applause and the start of the overture, the answer was contained in the music itself.

The great chords came, the huge theatrical announcement faded, became eerie and wavering, turned to dancing, and strutting, boastful little adventures. She had only seen *Don Giovanni* once, played by a travelling opera company with a reduced cast and a piano accompaniment on a fit-up set when she was at university. But she listened to the tapes often and knew the story of which they would hear no more than the overture. Now, as their hands locked, she looked at Jason's profile, clearly defined and sharp, the face of some particularly handsome bird of prey under untidy hair, and thought that the music of the man he had called 'The irresistible Don' added a good deal to the excitement of the occasion.

How could a man who was clearly guilty of murdering the Commendatore and raping his daughter, who exploited his servants and treated his former mistresses extremely badly, provoke fascination even as an opera's anti-hero? She thought about this as the overture ended with a final flourish, the conductor jerked and bowed and the promenaders stamped their approval. And then, after the piano had been wheeled into position and the concerto had begun, Selina thought that the Don had one redeeming moment. It was carelessly brave, wasn't it, to invite the statue of his murder victim to dinner? The scene in the graveyard had, had it not, a sort of splendour to it? And his amused behaviour when his ghostly visitor arrived with a blast of icy air and orders to repent had to be admired. By now Jason's fingers had unwound themselves from hers, and his hand was resting, gently possessive, an inch above her knee. Devoted to the music as she was, she began to wonder what she should order for dinner in the Italian restaurant at the other end of Kensington High Street, which he had described to her, and in what strange bedroom she would finally awake.

THERE WERE FIVE OTHER COUPLES in the box enjoying Clarion's corporate hospitality and, in the interval, they gathered in a room opposite the boxes for a glass of wine and a discussion of schools for their children, extensions to their cottages in the country and even, in some cases, the music. There was a jovial man who handled the advertising account of Fieldfare Foods, whose commercials regularly appeared on Clarion, and his small, active wife who buzzed from couple to couple offering nuts and bright contributions to flagging conversations. There was a grey-haired man who placed advertisements for cars and who had taken a deep and unexpected pleasure in the concerto; his large wife smiled a great deal, panted slightly and called Selina 'dear'. There was a tall, discontented-looking young man in a collarless shirt, an unstructured suit and a single earring, who directed the commercials where the cars were seen flying through the air, climbing impossible mountains or pursuing beautiful girls through the market in Marrakesh, visual images so brilliant that it was hard to remember which type of car was being advertised. His sullen girlfriend wondered why concerts had to drag up the music of dead, white, male composers. There was the Chairman of the Clarion board who treated Jason like a father with a peculiarly brilliant son, and his wife who asked Selina if she didn't find it quite impossible to keep more than one dog in London. There was a Japanese couple who smiled a great deal and a nervous Head of Comedy who, Jason had told her, was to be sacked the next morning. Selina didn't know how many of these guests might have seen Jason's hand resting above her knee, and, if she had to be honest, she didn't greatly care. Undoubtedly he was the star of the occasion. As he approached each couple they seemed to become livelier and to enjoy the evening more for his presence. And Selina, as his chosen partner, felt their approval and a kind of envy. 'My dear,' one of the wives breathed at her through a mouthful of potato crisps, 'isn't he looking particularly gorgeous tonight?' And she had to agree.

'Well,' Jason returned to her. 'What about that magnificent overture?'

'Wonderful. I wish we could have had the whole opera.'

'The love affair with the peasant girl. The escape from the masked ball and dinner with the statue. You wanted all *that*, did you?'

'Every bit of it!' The other guests were listening, moving nearer to hear Jason's verdict on the music.

'Just imagine,' he said, 'old Mozart sitting down to write that overture, knowing he had all the rest to do, all that great music to get out of his system. The Champagne Aria. The list of lovers… Everything ahead of him. It must have been pretty daunting!'

'It would have been,' Selina agreed. 'Only of course it didn't happen like that.'

'What do you mean?' She didn't, at first, notice his look of displeasure. She had not only read the notes that came with her tapes but also at least one 'life' of her favourite composer. She thought, at that moment, that he'd be glad to know. 'Actually Mozart wrote the overture last. After he'd finished the whole opera. Most composers do.'

'Oh, I don't think so.' Jason was looking down at her, smiling, as though she were a particularly silly child. 'Overture means opening, doesn't it? The beginning. The start of the affair.'

She had said nothing when he had mistaken Mozart for Schubert, but now it was her evening, she was full of confidence and anxious to tell him something she thought he'd be glad to know. 'You remember that the first night of *Don Giovanni* was in Prague...?'

'Was it really?' He was smiling at his guests but not at her. 'Perhaps we ought to be getting back...'

'No. It's a great story. The night before the opening. He was at a party, enjoying himself. He was writing a song for his hostess and he hadn't composed a note of the overture.'

'I don't think that's very likely.' Jason looked round at his audience, who apparently agreed with him. 'Anyway, I think we'll save the lecture till later.'

Anger, for Selina, was a rare experience. She had two parents who loved her. She'd passed easily from school to university and for most of her life she had kept reasonably calm. But now she was being patronised, when she only had a record to put right and an interesting story. She was determined to tell it.

'He went up to his room at midnight. Got his wife to make him punch and stay to keep him awake. He'd finished the opera by the morning.'

'Not much fun for Mrs Mozart, then.' The audience laughed obediently.

'It's true though!' She felt her cheeks burning and her voice become louder than she intended. 'Only the copyists couldn't work as fast as he did. The audience was kept waiting for an hour until the orchestra's parts arrived. And when the pages came they were covered in sand.'

'You mean he'd taken a quick trip to the seaside?'

'No! They used sand instead of blotting paper.' She was surprised at how angry she sounded.

'Well,' Jason was looking at her and now she found his boyish grin maddening. 'I don't know what you've been reading. One of those historical bodice rippers? "The Sex and Symphonies of Wolfgang Amadeus"? Come on, my group. Let's not miss the symphony. I suppose we're going to hear he wrote that backwards?'

Again his audience laughed and Jason moved towards the door which was open on to the corridor of boxes. An elderly woman, apparently lost, was standing in the doorway. Selina thought how pale she was. There seemed to be a sort of unearthly whiteness about her face and hair. She wore a blue dress with a shawl around her shoulders and rested, as though lame, on a black ebony walking stick. She was looking at Jason, apparently in amazement, and called his name. Her voice came, Selina thought when she remembered it all, with a hint of a mid-European accent.

'Marika.' Jason stopped smiling as he said it.

'You're with friends,' the woman told him as though he hadn't realised it. 'I'm afraid I got lost. So confusing, all these corridors.' She turned and rested a moment on her stick, and was then back in the crowds in the corridor.

'See you later,' Jason called after her, and added, for Selina's benefit, 'or sometime.'

'Who was that?'

He answered her quietly, as the others moved away. 'My wife, actually. We haven't been together for years. She was always older than me. Although she was quite beautiful once,' he added, as though it were an excuse.

'See you in a minute,' Selina told him, and made for the door. She hadn't forgiven him, nor would she ever.

∞

THE CORRIDOR THAT LED BEHIND the circle of boxes was crowded, but the woman with the black ebony walking stick was moving so slowly that Selina soon caught up with her.

'Excuse me, Mrs Tench. I'm your husband's PA.'

'I'm not sure where I came from.' The white face and pale eyes were turned towards her. 'Am I on the wrong floor?'

'Don't worry, Mrs Tench.' Selina was smiling. 'Your husband wants you to join him in his box. There's a free seat. If you're alone...'

'Oh yes, I am,' the woman assured her. 'Quite alone.'

'Then it's Box 18. Let me show you the way.'

In sight of the box, Selina left Mrs Tench to go on alone. She walked slowly but remorselessly, pausing occasionally to lean upon her stick.

Later Selina joined the promenaders. She was on the crowded floor where she had sat as a child, among the legs of the music lovers as her mother stood above her, humming along with some much loved symphony. Looking back at the boxes she saw Jason peering anxiously round the Albert Hall. Beside him his wife, the unexpected guest, sat motionless, pale as a ghost.

Selina turned from them and was soon lost in the opening bars of the *Jupiter*.

THE
DANCING-
MASTER'S
MUSIC

William Trevor

∾∾∾

BRIGID'S PROVINCE WAS THE SCULLERIES, which was where you began if you were a girl, the cutlery room and the bootroom if you weren't. Brigid began when she was fourteen and she was still fourteen when she heard about the dancing-master. It was Mr Crome who talked about him first, whose slow, lugubrious delivery came through the open scullery door from the kitchen. Lily Geoghegan said Mr Crome gave you a sermon whenever he opened his mouth.

'An Italian person, we are to surmise. From the Italian city of Naples. A travelling person.'

'Well, I never,' Mrs O'Brien interjected, and Brigid could tell she was busy with something else.

The sculleries were low-ceilinged, with saucepans and kettles hanging on pot-hooks, and the bowls and dishes and jelly-moulds which weren't often in use crowding the long shelf that continued from one scullery to the next even though there was a doorway between the two. Years ago the door that belonged in it had been taken off its hinges because it was in the way, but the hinges were left behind, too stiff to move now. Flanked with wide draining-boards, four slate sinks stretched beneath windows that had bars on the outside, and when the panes weren't misted Brigid could see the yard sheds and the pump. Once in a while one of the garden boys drenched the cobbles with buckets of water and swept them clean.

'Oh, yes,' Mr Crome went on. 'Oh, yes, indeed. That city famed in fable.'

'Is it Italian steps he's teaching them, Mr Crome?'

'Austria is the source of the steps, we have to surmise. I hear Vienna mentioned. Another city of renown.'

Mr Crome's sermon began then, the history of the waltz step, and Brigid didn't listen. From the sound of the range dampers being adjusted, the oven door opened and closed, she could tell that Mrs O'Brien wasn't listening either.

Nobody listened much to Mr Crome when he got going, when he wasn't cross, when he wasn't giving out about dust between the banister supports or the fires not right or a staleness on the water of the carafes. You listened then all right, no matter who you were.

Every morning, early, Brigid walked from Glenmore, over Skenakilla Hill to Skenakilla House. She waited at the back door until John or Thomas opened it. If Mr Crome kept her on, if she gave satisfaction and was conscientious, if her disposition in the sculleries turned out to be agreeable, she would lodge in. Mr Crome had explained that, using those words and expressions. She was glad she didn't have to live in the house immediately.

Brigid was tall for her age, surprising Mr Crome when she told him what it was. Fair-haired and freckled, she was the oldest of five, a country girl from across the hill. 'Nothing much in the way of looks,' Mr Crome confided in the kitchen after he'd interviewed her. Her mother he remembered well, for she had once worked in the sculleries herself, but unfortunately had married Stranahan instead of advancing in her employment, and was now – so Mr Crome passed on to Mrs O'Brien – brought low by poverty and childbirth. Stranahan was never sober.

Brigid was shy in the sculleries at first. The others glanced in when they passed, or came to look at her if they weren't pressed. When they spoke to her she could feel a warmth coming into her face and the more she was aware of it the more it came, confusing her, sometimes making her say what she didn't intend to say. But when a few weeks had gone by all that was easier, and by the time the dancing-master arrived in the house she didn't even find dinner time the ordeal it had been at first.

'Where's Naples, Mr Crome?' Thomas asked in the kitchen dining-room on the day Mr Crome first talked about Italy. 'Where'd it be placed on the map, Mr Crome?'

He was trying to catch Mr Crome out. Brigid could see Annie-Kate looking away in case she giggled, and Lily Geoghegan's elbow nudged by the tip of John's. Nodding and smiling between her mouthfuls, deaf to all that was said, but with flickers of ancient beauty still alive in her features, old Mary sat at the other end of the long table at which Mr Crome presided. Beside him, Mrs O'Brien saw that he was never without mashed potato on his plate specially mashed, for Mr Crome would not eat potatoes served otherwise. The Widow Kinawe, who came on Mondays and Thursdays for the washing and was sometimes on the back avenue when Brigid reached it in the mornings, sat next to her at the table, with Jerety from the garden on the other side, and the garden boys beside him.

'Naples is washed by the sea,' Mr Crome said.

'I'd say I heard a river mentioned, Mr Crome. It wouldn't be a river it's washed by?' 'What you heard, boy, was the River Danube. Nowhere near.' And Mr Crome traced the course of that great river, taking a chance here and there in his version of its itinerary. It was a river that gave its name to a waltz, which would be why Thomas heard it mentioned.

'Well, that beats Banagher!' Mrs O'Brien said.

Mrs O'Brien often said that. In the dining-room next to the kitchen the talk was usually of happenings in the house, of arrivals and departures, news received, announcements made, anticipations: Mrs O'Brien's expression of wonderment was regularly called upon. John and Thomas, or the two bedroom maids, or Mr Crome himself, brought from the upper rooms the harrowings left behind after drawing-room conversation or dining-room exchanges, or chatter anywhere at all. 'Harrowings' was Mrs O'Brien's word, servitude's share of the household's chatter.

∾

IT WAS WINTER WHEN BRIGID BEGAN in the sculleries and when the dancing-master came to the house. Every evening she would return home across the hill in the dark, but after the first few times she knew the way well, keeping to the stony track, grateful when there was moonlight. She took with her, once in four weeks, the small wage Mr Crome paid her, not expecting more until she was trained in the work. When it rained she managed as best she could, drying her clothes in the hearth when she got home, the fire kept up for that purpose. When it rained in the mornings she could feel the dampness pressed on her all day.

The servants were what Brigid knew of Skenakilla House. She heard about the Master and Mrs Everard and the family, about Miss Turpin and Miss Roche, and the grandeur of the furniture and the rooms. She imagined them, but she had not ever seen them. The reality of the servants when they sat down together at dinner time she brought home across Skenakilla

Hill: long-faced Thomas, stout John, Old Mary starting conversations that nobody kept going, Lily Geoghegan and Annie-
Kate giggling into their food, the lugubriousness of Mr Crome,
Mrs O'Brien flushed and flurried when she was busy. She told of
the disappointments that marked the widowhood of the Widow
Kinawe, of Jerety wordless at the dinner table, his garden boys
silent also.

'Ah, he's no size at all. Thin as a knife-blade,' was the hearsay
that Brigid took across Skenakilla Hill when the dancing-
master arrived. 'Black hair, like Italians have. A shine to it.'

At one and the same time he played the piano and taught the
steps, Mr Crome said, and recalled another dancing-master, a
local man from the town, who had brought a woman to play the
piano and a fiddler to go with her. Buckley, that man was called,
coming out to the house every morning in his own little cart,
with his retinue.

'Though for all that,' Mr Crome said, 'I doubt he had the
style of the Italian man. I doubt Buckley had the bearing.'

Once Brigid heard the music, a tinkling of the piano keys
that lasted only as long as the green, baize-covered door at the
end of the kitchen passage was open. John's shoulder held it
wide while he passed through with a tray of cups and saucers.
At the time, Annie-Kate was showing Brigid how to fill the oil
lamps in the passage, which soon would become one of her
duties if Mr Crome decided she was satisfactory. Until that
morning she had never been in the passage before, the sculleries
being on the other side of the kitchen wing. 'That same old
tune,' Annie-Kate said. 'He never leaves it.' But Brigid would
have listened for longer and was disappointed when the baize
door closed and the sound went with it. It was the first time she
had heard a piano played.

Three days later, at dinner time, Mr Crome said: 'The Italian has done with them. On Friday he'll pack his traps and go on to Skibbereen.'

'Can they do the steps now, Mr Crome?' Annie-Kate asked, in the pert manner she sometimes put on at the dinner table when she forgot herself.

'That is not for us to know,' Mrs O'Brien reprimanded her, but Mr Crome pondered the question. It was a safe assumption, he suggested eventually, that the dancing-master wouldn't be leaving unless the purpose of his visit had been fulfilled. He interrupted a contribution on the subject from John to add:

'It's not for that I mention it. On Thursday night he is to play music to us.'

'What d'you mean, Mr Crome?' Mrs O'Brien was startled by the news, and Brigid remembered hearing Lily Geoghegan once whispering to Annie-Kate that Mrs O'Brien was put out when she wasn't told privately and in advance anything of importance in Mr Crome's news.

'I'll tell you what I mean, Mrs O'Brien. It's that every man jack of us will sit down upstairs, that John and Thomas will carry up to the drawing-room the chairs we are occupying this minute and arrange them as directed by myself, that music will be played for us.'

'Why's that, Mr Crome?' Annie-Kate asked.

'It's what has been arranged, Annie. It's what we're being treated to on Thursday evening.'

'We're never sitting down with the Master and Mrs Everard? With the girls and Miss Turpin and Miss Roche? You're having us on, Mr Crome!' Annie-Kate laughed and Lily Geoghegan laughed, and John and Thomas. Old Mary joined in.

But Mr Crome had never had anyone on in his life. For the

purpose of the dancing-master's recital, the drawing-room would be vacated by the family, he explained. The family would have heard the music earlier that same day, in the late afternoon. It was a way of showing gratitude to the dancing-master for his endeavours that he was permitted to give his performance a second time.

'Is it the stuff he's always hammering out we'll have to listen to?' Annie-Kate asked. 'The waltz steps, is it, Mr Crome?'

Mr Crome shook his head. He had it personally from Miss   57
Turpin that the music selected by the dancing-master was different entirely. It was music that was suitable for the skill he possessed at the piano, not composed by himself yet he knew every note off by heart and didn't need to read off a page.

'Well, I never!' Mrs O'Brien marvelled, mollified because all that Mr Crome said by way of explanation had been directly addressed to her, irrespective of where the queries came from.

∽

ON THAT THURSDAY EVENING, although Brigid didn't see the Master or Mrs Everard, or the girls, or Miss Turpin or Miss Roche, she saw the drawing-room. At the end of a row, next to the Widow Kinawe, she took her place on one of the round-bottomed chairs that had been arranged at Mr Crome's instruction, and looked about her. A fire blazed at either end of the long, shadowy room and, hanging against blue-striped wallpaper, there were gilt-framed portraits, five on one wall, four on another. There were lamps on the mantelpiece and on tables, a marble figure in a corner, the chairs and the sofa the family sat on all empty now. A grand piano had pride of place.

Brigid had never seen a portrait before. She had never seen such furniture, or two fires in a room. She had never seen a piano, grand or otherwise. On the wide boards of the floor, rugs were spread, and in a whisper the Widow Kinawe drew her attention to the ceiling, which was encrusted with a pattern of leaves and flowers, all in white.

Small, and thin as a knife-blade, just as she had described him herself, the dancing-master brought with him a scent of oil when he arrived, a lemony smell yet with a sweetness to it. He entered the drawing-room, closed the door behind him, and went quickly to the piano, not looking to either side of him. He didn't speak, but sat down at once, clasped his hands together, splayed his fingers, exercising them before he began. All the time he played the music, the scent of oil was there, subtle in the warm air of the drawing-room.

There had been a fiddler at the wake of Brigid's grandmother. He was an old man who suffered from the coldness, who sat close in to the hearth and played a familiar dirge and then another and another. There was keening and after it the tuneless sound continued, the fiddler hunched over the glow of the turf, Brigid's grandmother with her hands crossed over her funeral dress in the other room. But while the lamplight flickered and the two fires blazed, the dancing-master's music was different in every way from the fiddler's. It scurried and hurried, softened, was calm, was slow. It danced over the striped-blue walls and the gaze of the portrait people. It lingered on the empty chairs, on vases and ornaments. It rose up to reach the white flowers of the encrusted ceiling. Brigid closed her eyes and the dancing-master's music crept about her darkness, its tunes slipping away, recalled, made different. There was the singing of a thrush. There was thunder far away, and the stream she went by on Skenakilla Hill, rushing, then babbling. The silence was different when the music stopped, as if the music had changed it.

The dancing-master stood up then and bowed to the congregated servants, who bowed back to him, not knowing what else to do. He left the drawing-room, still without saying anything, and the round-bottomed chairs were carried back to where they'd come from. Brigid caught a glimpse of John and Lily Geoghegan kissing while she was getting herself ready for the walk across the hill. 'Well, there's skill in it all right,' was Mr Crome's verdict on the dancing-master's performance, but Thomas said he'd thought they'd hear a few jigs and Annie-Kate complained she'd nearly died, sitting on a hard chair for an hour and a half. The Widow Kinawe said it was great to see inside a room the like of that, twenty-three pieces of china she'd counted. Old Mary hadn't heard a thing, but still declared she'd never spent a better evening. 'Who was that man at all?' she asked Mrs O'Brien, whose eyes had closed once or twice, but not as Brigid's had.

That February night on the stony hillside track there was frost in the air and the sky was blazing with stars that seemed to Brigid to be a further celebration of the music she'd heard, of beauty and of a feeling in herself. The tunes she tried for eluded her, but somehow it was right that they should, that you couldn't just reach out for them. The hurrying and the slowness and the calm, the music made of the stream she walked by now, were vague and uncertain. But crossing Skenakilla Hill, she took with her enough of what there had been, and it was still enough when she woke in the morning, and still enough when she worked again in the sculleries.

Mr Crome said at dinner time that the dancing-master had left the house after breakfast. One last time he'd gone through the waltz steps. Then he left for Skibbereen.

∾

THAT NIGHT, BRIGID DREAMED she went with him. She dreamed of a town she had never seen, of other rooms in which the music was played, of being the dancing-master's servant, attending to his clothes, always with him when his music began. Varying a little, this dream returned on other nights, often at first and then only once in a while. But for all Brigid's life she never ceased to dream about the dancing-master.

While other incidents and occurrences marked the years that slipped by, during heatwaves and frozen winters, when spring came again, and the storms of another autumn, the evening in the drawing-room remained with Brigid, privately and her own, as her dreaming was. Advancing in her employment, she came to know the house and the family. She shared a bedroom with Lily Geoghegan and Annie-Kate, who grumbled about it. On Sunday afternoons she walked home on the track and in the solitude of Skenakilla Hill she remembered the stars of that February night and how they had seemed like a celebration. Sometimes at Mass, when the Host was offered, she saw the dancing-master's small, lean face and wondered if he'd died, and prayed for him. Once in her dream his coffin was taken from a house, and she felt him thanking her for her prayers, while his music played for her.

Often in the time that passed, while Brigid moved out of her girlhood, while no man loved her as John loved Lily Geoghegan, while she aged in the place of her work, she heard the piano played in the drawing-room. She always stopped whatever she was doing in another room to listen, hearing with pleasure the sound that came to her, even when it was jagged or suddenly broke off and had to begin again. But nothing haunted her in what she heard, nothing stayed with her, even vaguely and uncertainly; nothing caused her to dream. Although at first she hoped she'd one day hear again the music of the dancing-master, she was glad in the end that it was not played by someone else. It was his and it was hers, no matter where it had come from or who had made it up. As old as Old Mary, long after there was no reason for her to cross the hill, since a room in the house had become her home, Brigid continued to walk on the stony track during the hours given back to her once a week as her own. And always, in the way that once had been enough and still was, the dancing-master's music was there with her, the marvel in her life.

BEEHERNZ

Penelope Fitzgerald

To Hopkins, deputy artistic director of the Midland
Music Festival, an idea came. Not a new idea, but
rather comforting in its familiarity, an idea for the
two opening concerts next year. He put it forward, not at the
preliminary meeting, still at quite an early one.

'Out of the question if it involves us in any further expense,'
said the chairman.

'No, it's a matter of concept,' said Hopkins. 'These are
Mahler concerts, agreed, and we need Mahler specialists.

I suggest that for the first one we book a young tearaway, no
shortage of those, and for the other a retired maestro – well, they
don't retire, but I have in mind a figure from the past making
one of his rare appearances, venerated, dug up for the occasion,
someone, perhaps, thought to be dead.'

He mentioned the name of Beehernz. Most of those present
had thought he was dead. Some of them remembered the name,
but did not get it quite right. It was thought he had something
to do with the 'Symphony of a Thousand'. In fact, however, he'd
had nothing to do with it. Nearly forty years earlier, in 1960,
the BBC had celebrated the centenary of Mahler's birth. It was
only at a very late stage that Beehernz, booked for the occasion,
had said, in his quiet way – that was how it had been described
to Hopkins, 'in his quiet way' – that he would prefer a

substitute to be found for him, since he had only just learned that he was expected to conduct the Eighth Symphony.

'What is your objection to the Eighth Symphony?' he was asked.

'It is too noisy,' replied Beehernz.

Beehernz had not appeared in public since that time. Hopkins's committee agreed that his name could be made into a talking point. Would Hopkins undertake the arrangements? Yes, everything, everything.

According to the BBC's records, Beehernz lived in Scotland and had done so since 1960 – not on the mainland, but on an island off an island – Reilig, off Iona, off Mull, via Oban.

'"Reilig" means "graveyard" in Gaelic,' said the BBC reference librarian.

'There's no regular ferry from Iona,' said the Scottish Tourist Board, 'but you can enquire at Fionnphort.'

Preliminaries were conducted by letter, because Beehernz was not on the telephone. Some of Hopkins's letters were answered, in not very firm handwriting. The contract too came back, signed, but still not pleasing to the festival's accounts manager. 'Where's the compensation clause? A specific sum should be named as a guarantee of his appearance… They can go missing at any age… Stokowski signed a ten-year recording contract at the age of ninety-five… It's worse as they get older, they just forget to turn up… It needn't be an immense sum… What does he live on, anyway?' Hopkins replied that he supposed Beehernz lived on his savings.

Hopkins was more interested in what the old maestro was going to play. Something, certainly, that wouldn't need more than two rehearsals, if possible only one.

'I'd better go and see him myself,' he said. This was what he had always had in mind.

He was going to take two other people with him. One was a singer, Mary Lockett. He didn't know her at all well, but she was only just starting on her career and wouldn't refuse – no one ever refused a free trip to Scotland. She had a 'white' voice, not really at all the kind of voice Mahler had liked himself, but she was said to be adaptable. Then he'd take his dogsbody from the Festival office, young Fraser. In the evening on the Isle of Reilig they would sit round the piano and let decisions grow. Hopkins couldn't decide whether he expected to find the old man seated, solipsistic, huddled in past memories, or nervously awaiting visitors, trembling in the overeagerness of welcome. Hopkins wrote to say they would arrive on the 21st of May, leaving the car in Oban.

'We'll do well to buy some supplies here,' said young Fraser. 'Mr Beehernz will very likely not have much in the house.'

They went to Oban's largest supermarket and bought tea, Celebrated Auld Style Shortbread, cold bacon, and, after some hesitation on Hopkins's part, a bottle of whisky. Half a bottle would look too calculated. He didn't know whether Mary Lockett took an occasional drink or not.

'There's always a first time,' said Fraser reassuringly.

They crossed to Mull, Fraser and Mary with their backpacks, Hopkins with his discreet travel-bag and document case. There was a message for them at Fionnphort, telling them to take the next ferry to Iona, and wait for McGregor. At Iona's jetty all the other day-trippers got out and began to walk off briskly, as though drilled, northward towards the Cathedral. Time passes more slowly in small places. After what was perhaps three-quarters of an hour, someone who was evidently McGregor came jolting towards them in a Subaru. They'd have to drive over, he said, to the west coast, where he kept his boat at moorings.

Iona is three miles long and one mile wide, and Reilig looked considerably smaller. The blue sky, cloudless that day, burned as if it was as salt as the water below them. There was no sand or white shell beach as you approached, and the rocky shoreline was not impressive, just enough to give you a nasty fall. There was a landing stage with a tarred shed beside it, and a paved track leading up to a small one-storey building of sorts.

'Is that Mr Beehernz's crofthouse?' Hopkins asked. McGregor replied that it was not a croft, but it was Beehernz's place.

'I imagine he's expecting us,' said Hopkins, although he felt it as a kind of weakness to appeal to McGregor, who told them that the door would be open and they'd best go in, but Beehernz might be there or he might be out on his potato patch. When he had seen them safely off the landing stage he disappeared into the shed, which was roofed with corrugated iron.

The front door was shut fast and weeds had grown as high as the lock. The door at the side was open, and led into a dark little hen-kitchen with just about enough room for a sink and a dresser and two dishevelled fowls who ran shrieking into the bright air outside. Fraser and Mary stood awkwardly by the sink, politeness suggesting to them to go no further.

'Beehernz!' Hopkins called. 'May we come in?'

I need absolutely to find out what he's really like. This is the opportunity before he comes back.

One step up into the living-room, white-washed, a clock ticking, no electricity, no radio, a single bed covered with a plaid, an armchair, no books, no bookcase, no scores, no manuscripts. Through into the kitchen, hardly bigger than a cupboard, a paraffin lamp waiting to be filled, a venerable bread crock, and, taking up half the space, a piano, a sad old mission-hall thing, still, a piano. Hopkins lifted the lid and tried the sagging middle C. It was silent. He played up the scale and down. No sound. Next door, the scullery and water-closet, fit for an antiquarian.

A disturbance in the hen-kitchen, where the two seedy fowls were rushing in again, revelling in their own panic. Mary and Fraser had just been joined by a third party, an old man who had taken off his gum-boots and was now concentrating all his attention on putting on his slippers.

67

'Ah, you must be...' said Hopkins. *But that's quite wrong. I don't want to sound as though I'm the host.*

Beehernz at length said, 'I am sorry, but you must let me rest a little. My health, such of it as remains, depends on my doing the same thing at the same time every day.'

He advanced with padding steps, a little, light old man, and sat down in the only chair. Hopkins and Fraser sat gingerly on the bed. Mary did not come into the living-room. She was still in the hen-kitchen, unfastening the backpacks and taking out the Celebrated Auld Style Shortbread, the cold bacon and the tea. She then began to take down the tin plates from the dresser. Mary never did anything in a hurry. As she moved about she could be heard singing, just quietly, from the middle of her voice, not paying any particular heed – it was a nursery tune in any case:

'Ich ging im Walde
So für mich hin,
Und nichts zu suchen,
Das war mein Sinn.

In Schatten sah ich
Ein Blumlein stehn –
Where am I to lay out the plates?'

Beehernz was on his feet. 'No, no, not now, not yet. Not yet. Let the young people go out for a little while.'

'But we brought…' Fraser said, in unconcealed disappointment.

'For a little while,' repeated Beehernz.

'Let me explain, Mr Hopkins. I would prefer Mr – er – and Miss – er – I would prefer them to go back to Iona with McGregor's boat. Yes, that is what I wish.'

'This is rather unexpected. I wrote to you, you remember, to tell you that there would be three of us coming.'

Beehernz passed his hands over his forehead and looked out from between them, as though playing some melancholy game.

'Three is too many, Mr Hopkins, to impose upon me so suddenly.'

What's come over him? He may have it in mind to push the two of them over the cliff's edge, two souls for whom I'm responsible to the festival committee.

'I'll go and see where they are.'

After all, they couldn't go far. They were sitting on a rocky outcrop, looking westward.

Fraser seemed to be silent, perhaps from hunger. Mary never said much at any time. She was twisting the straw handle of her shopping bag between her fingers. Why did women always have to carry bags about with them?

Hopkins made his explanation. An old man's fancy. They mustn't, of course, take it personally.

'How else can we take it?' Fraser asked.

'You'll be able to get accommodation on Iona, perhaps at the Abbey.'

'Will there be room?'

'Well, perhaps you'll find they've taken some vow not

to turn away travellers in an emergency. You must both of you get someone to sign your expenses and keep them in duplicate, of course.'

'Surely we ought to say a few words of thanks to Mr Beehernz,' said Fraser.

'No, no, you've nothing to thank him for, you'd better go and put your things together.' McGregor, indeed, was advancing up the path, saying that if there was anyone for the return journey, they would want to be getting into the boat.

As the boat ticked away through the calm and sparkling water, Fraser seemed to be shouting something. Sound is always said to carry well over water. This didn't. He'd taken something, or mistaken something. Mary's back was turned, as though on an experience that was over and done with.

When he got back he found Beehernz methodically chewing the cold bacon. 'Sit down, Mr Hopkins. I eat once a day only, usually in the evening. But if it turns out to be midday, so be it.'

And the whisky, what's he done with that? Hopkins realised then what Fraser must have been calling from the boat. He'd taken the bag with the whisky with him, in error, no doubt. The tape recorder was in it, too; Hopkins was left without his standbys, old and new.

'Perhaps you would like to see my potato-bed,' said Beehernz presently. 'I depend on it very extensively. My hens have not laid for nearly a year, although I have not quite lost hope.'

They walked up the gently rising ground to the south, past a washing line from which a long-sleeved vest idly flapped, to an open patch of soil surrounded by a low stone wall. Here Beehernz explained his time-honoured way of cultivating his crop, describing it as a traditional West Highland method. He

didn't bury the seed potatoes, but laid them in rows on the surface and dug trenches between the rows, covering them with
earth from the trenches as he did so. McGregor had shown him
how to do that, or, to be more accurate, McGregor's father.

'Nothing's come up yet,' said Hopkins.

'No, not a green leaf showing.' They stood listening to the
gulls crying from every side of them, high up in the deafening
blue.

70 'Why did you try out my piano this morning?' Beehernz
asked.

You old wretch, you old monster, how do you know I did?

Back in the living-room, Hopkins brought the piano stool
out of the kitchen and drew it up to the table. Then he opened
up his document case, moving aside the remnants of the cold
food. On this island of Reilig he felt authority leaving him,
with no prospect of being replaced by anything else. Authority
was scarcely needed in a kingdom of potatoes and seabirds.

I'll begin, he thought, *by calling him by his first name*, then
found he had forgotten it. Temporarily of course – he was
under stress.

He went on, 'I respect your privacy, and I'm sure you understand that.'

Beehernz replied that he had never considered it at all.
'You need two people to respect privacy, or, indeed, to make
it necessary.'

Hopkins took a selection of documents out of his case. Doing
this reassured him. The name was Konrad, of course.

'This is our copy of the original contract. You have had your
copy signed and returned to you. It didn't at any time specify
what your programme was to include. Now, although this
wasn't my main object in coming, I've been turning a few

thoughts over in my mind, just to see how they strike you.'
Beehernz simply repeated the word 'thoughts' with an inappropriate laugh (it was the first time he had laughed). Hopkins
continued, 'I take it that you don't, and never did, want to present the monumental Mahler. As I see it, you might begin with
some of the early songs – let's say the *Lieder eines fahrenden
Gesellen*, the 1884 version, with the piano accompaniment...'

Beehernz shook his head slightly with a particularly sweet
smile, which, however, wasn't apologetic, rather it dismissed
the whole subject.

'Who was that young woman who was here recently?'
he asked.

'You mean Mary Lockett. She was here this morning. So, for
that matter, was my assistant Fraser. You told me that you
would like them both to leave.'

'I assumed that if they came together, they would prefer to
leave together.'

'That was a total misunderstanding. They're no more than
acquaintances.'

'A thousand pardons.'

He's not of sound mind – reflected Hopkins. *In that case the
contract is void anyway*. He said: 'Am I to understand, then, that
you simply don't want to discuss the subject of Mahler?'

Beehernz smiled still. With a show of determination,
Hopkins put another set of papers in front of him, and saw him
dutifully bend over them.

After twenty minutes, after which he only appeared to be at
paragraph two, Beehernz looked up and asked:

'If I die, or even become seriously ill, before conducting this
concert, who will be liable to pay this large sum?' He had
understood nothing.

'No one would be liable for that,' said Hopkins. It would be *force majeure*.'

Beehernz put both his hands down flat on the papers, as if to eliminate them from his sight. 'Well, I will think about it.'

'Couldn't you decide now?'

'Formerly I could have done so, but now I can only think of one thing at a time.'

Then what are you thinking about now, you old charlatan, you old crook.

'By the way, don't distress yourself about how you are going to get away from the island. McGregor will be back tomorrow. It will be his regular delivery day, when he brings me my few necessities from Iona.'

'What time does he come?'

'He will knock on the door.'

'What time?'

'Early, early, at first light. After that I do not expect him back for another two weeks.'

Hopkins spent the night in the armchair, which, after years of accommodating Beehernz, resolutely refused to fit anyone else. Since there were no bedclothes in the place beyond the plaid, he slept in his shirt and jacket. It was still dark when he suggested putting on the kettle. Beehernz, apparently spry and wakeful, told him that he had never possessed a kettle. 'That may interest you. We never had one, even when I was a child in Leipzig.' He sighed, and went to sleep again. But when the sky grew light, when the unshaven Hopkins had opened the door to McGregor, who said he didn't want tea, thanks, he'd made some in the shed – just as well, Hopkins thought – Beehernz appeared, wearing a tattered *Regenhaut* and a wide-brimmed hat. He was ready not only to go out, but to go away.

'I shall accompany you.'

'You didn't say anything about this last night.'

'I should like to hear that young woman sing again. She cannot have got any further than Iona.'

'You sent her away.'

'I have changed my mind. I should like to hear her sing again. You see, it is so long since I heard music.'

SHELL SONGS

Clare Boylan

A T FIVE DAMIAN WAS AT THE WINDOW. The sky was like a sail, soft and billowy white. The water was creased with sleep. Three birds floated overhead, their wings touching so that they seemed to be holding hands. They flung out their cries loud enough for him to hear. He thought they must be sisters.

Apart from the birds, he was the only one awake. He scoured the horizon like Robinson Crusoe. He wasn't looking for a ship. He was searching for a ray of light. All month it had been the same, the silvery dawns and blustery days, his mother leaning on the window sill, blowing smoke at the mist on the window and then wiping both away.

'When can I go out?' He should have brought his wellington boots. Maybe then she wouldn't mind about the weather.

'When the rain stops,' she'd say for the hundredth time.

The rain wouldn't bother him. You got wet in the sea so it hardly mattered if the sky made you wet as well. 'If my father was here he'd take me out,' he'd say.

'Fat lot your father cares,' she'd mutter.

He woke an hour later, disturbed by the light. He was still at the window in his pyjamas. Then he gave a shudder of excitement. The sun was shining. The sky was blue all over. He ran to tell his mother, but she was fast asleep so that her face and her hair seemed to be melting on the pillow. He pulled on his shoes and jumper over the pyjamas and slipped out the door. The whole of the seaside was his. The beach hummed with its own brightness. He held out his arms and ran along the strand. His father did care. He had rented the cottage for him and his mother. The sea air would do them good, he said. He had told Damian he would go brown as a berry, although Damian had to point out that berries were usually red. 'As brown as a coffee bean, then,' his father said; 'Although, in fact, you are more likely to go red.'

When he was tired of running he took off his shoes and put his socks inside them and waded in the water. When he'd first arrived there was hardly any water, just an expanse of flat damp sand that was divided from the sky by a dark band of distant grey, but when he'd woken the following morning the tide was in. He was astonished by the size and laziness of the ocean, the way it shook its frills and whispered.

He closed his eyes and listened to that sound, the constant 'shh' that was like a lullaby. He knew now the sea was where he belonged. His mother would soon grow restless and want to move on. That was how it always was. His father probably wouldn't know where to find them. He thought it wouldn't be so bad if only he could take the sea home with him, hear its soothing 'shh' each time he closed his eyes. He knew that was stupid. He was always being told not to be a dreamer. When he opened his eyes he got a fright. The cottage had vanished. The beach had turned into a desert island.

From a long way off he saw a figure, black and forky as a winter tree. A dog waddled by its side and there was a horse and cart. 'Man Friday,' he breathed in excitement. 'Ahoy there!' he called and he waved his arms. The dog's bark had a metallic echo in this deserted world. The man made no response. When he got closer, Damian saw that he was not black, merely weathered brown, and that he had not heard him calling because he was wearing earphones.

'I'm lost,' Damian shouted.

'I'm Tewke!' The man pulled out an earpiece and grinned. 'You can't get lost on a beach. It goes one way and then it goes the other.'

'I've never been on a beach before.' Damian felt abashed.

'You the man from Mars?'

'I'm from the city.' Damian peered into the cart, at the writhing brown fronds with their rank and salty smell. 'Are you from here?'

'I'm from everywhere,' Tewke said.

'Are you a sailor?' Damian wondered, since sailors went with the sea.

'Tinker, tailor, soldier, sailor,' Tewke said; 'I do a bit of everything.'

'My father can do anything,' Damian told him. 'He's wizard!'

'Wizard!' The man seemed to chew on the word and then spit it out like a lump of used tobacco. 'You really are from Mars. What can he do?'

'He can make music,' Damian said. 'He can make money.'

'I made this cart myself.' Tewke slapped the wooden carriage with a rough hand. 'I could even make one for you. I've been collecting this from the beach.' He dug his hand into the cart and pulled out a handful of slippery frills.

'What is it?' Damian said.

'Neptune's manure. Fertilizer from the ocean floor. Full of iodine. I sell it to farmers. The sea's full of secrets.'

Damian felt excited by this exchange with the tall brown

man. Neptune's manure. He put the information away carefully. He loved his mother but one needed other men for knowledge. The thought of his mother reminded him that she would be awake by now and might be anxious. 'I should be getting back,' he said.

'Where you staying?'

'We're at Broom Cottage.'

'Yuppies!' the man laughed. 'If I take you back will I get a reward?'

'You would if my father was here.' Damian bent to pat the fat dog, which lounged against him, angling for a scratch. 'He's away making money.'

'So, it's you and your Ma? Pretty, is she? Maybe she'd give me a reward.'

This time Damian didn't like the way the man laughed.

'You want me to show you something?' Tewke put his hand in his pocket. 'I can show you something no one else can.'

'My father told me not to talk to strangers,' Damian began to walk away.

'Mermaid music!' Tewke came after him. 'Bet your Pa can't do that?' Mermaid music! Damian felt confused. There was something teasing about the man. He tossed the shell in the air. Damian watched its freckled surface gleaming in the sun. His own eyes were speckled when he looked down again, and it was a moment or two before he saw that there was someone else on the beach, her blonde hair pulled by the wind, her long cardigan hugged around her.

'Mam!' he cried and he ran as fast as his legs would carry him.

'Where've you been?' She stamped towards him. 'I've been walking miles looking for you.'

'I've been…' Damian looked around for his new ally, but he

had left him far behind. Already he seemed a remote feature of the landscape.

'Where's your shoes and socks?'

He looked down and saw with surprise that his feet were bare, and blue.

She took his footwear from behind her back. 'What was I supposed to think when I found these on the beach? I thought you were drowned, you stupid little twit.' She took his hand and dragged him all the way back to the cottage. 'You stay indoors until you've learnt your lesson.'

What lesson was he to learn? He gazed at the sea but it had grown dull and silent behind the dusty window. There was no school at the seaside so he would have to choose his own lesson. A music lesson he decided. He liked music – not the dance music his mother played on the radio, but soaring music. He had taken after his father in that. He couldn't get over the idea of mermaid music, though. What sort of sound would mermaids make? Something on a stringed instrument, maybe, not a violin or a harp but the one that was shaped like a 'u' with curly bits on the top. That would suit their shape. Or perhaps they would sing. A piping song came into his head – 'Songs of the Auvergne'. When his father had played it, he thought it didn't sound quite human. His father did not say what The Auvergne was. Maybe it was a tribe of mermaids.

The following morning he was out early, before his mother was awake. While he waited for Tewke he wrote his name in the sand with a stick and then drew long lines on either side, decorating them with shells to form a runway. Maybe his father would be flying overhead and would see his name.

When his mother appeared she was wearing her overcoat. She said she'd like to see the village now the weather had brightened. 'Let me stay,' Damian pleaded, but she told him not to be a pest. She wasn't having him wandering off alone again.

Why was he alone? He had imagined the beach would be full of children, that he would join with them in building a giant fortress in the sand, with moats and flags.

'We're early, is all. We don't want to get caught up with riff-raff.' His mother laughed, although Damian couldn't see the joke.

80 From the village he caught glimpses of the sea. He kept thinking of Tewke. Riff-raff. That must be the stuff Tewke collected in his cart. His mother looked at magazines and bought some groceries. In a seaside boutique she tried on jeans and a tee shirt. She went for a coffee then, and smoked some cigarettes, reading a magazine she had bought. Damian blew listlessly into a lemonade with his straw.

When they got back there was something on the doorstep. His mother picked up the small, roughly-carved figure of a horse. It had a little cart attached, and wheels that went around. 'Someone's left their toy.' She looked uncomfortable. She didn't care for strangers. 'It's rubbish,' she added, because it hadn't come from a shop.

'It's mine!' Damian could hardly speak for excitement. 'It's a present from Mr Tewke.' He tried to catch his breath, to stop himself from gabbling. 'He can do anything. He knows how to make music out of shells.'

'Liar!' His mother swept the horse out of reach.

'It's not a lie.' Tewke stepped out from the side of the cottage. He seemed different to yesterday, his hair combed and a fresh shirt on.

'Who are you when you're at home?' his mother looked him up and down.

'Tewke!' Damian exclaimed.

'Aren't you going to introduce me?' Tewke said.

'It's my Mam! Tell her, Tewke! You made the horse and cart for me.' Tewke nodded. Damian held his breath, for his mother could be blunt, but she didn't say anything, just watched him doubtfully and pulled at a strand of her hair.

'Can I go out with Mr Tewke?' Damian said.

'I'd need a word with him first,' his mother decided.

'That's right,' Tewke spoke very gently. He kept his eye on   81
Damian's mother although he addressed the boy. 'You go and play with your horse.'

'Can I, mother?' Damian said.

After all the fuss over the rain, he was surprised at the indifferent way in which she nodded. He ran down to the shore. He wanted to put something in the cart. He thought he would fill it with the small pearly shells he had used on his runway.

∞

'WHAT'S YOUR NAME?' Cobwebs made a sticky fizz as Tewke swept them from the doorway.

'I'm supposed to be asking the questions.' She went in and perched on the edge of a battered table.

'Ah, yes, but you know my name.' He sat beside her, leaned close, and she saw his bare brown throat. 'Niamh,' she said.

'Where's your husband, Niamh?' Tewke took cigarettes and matches from his pocket. He put a smoke in her mouth and lit her up.

'I haven't got one.'

When he shook the match out he let his hand rest on her knee. 'Where's the kid's father, then?'

'God knows.'

'He seems to know.'

'He's got a big imagination. Drives me round the bend. He's invented a father, like a sort of imaginary playmate. Doesn't mix with other kids, just reads them old-fashioned school books. I blame that teacher in his school, Mr Mooney, filling the kids' heads with rubbish. Instead of teaching them how to read and write, he plays records and reads books to them – fancy stuff.'

'What are you doing in this godforsaken gaff in the middle of winter? The rats have been paying the rent for the past year.'

'Hanging out. Squatting. I had a bit of trouble from a guy. He had a temper. Took it out on the kid.'

'That where he got those bruises?'

'You're too nosey. Like the damn social workers.'

'And you're getting sharp around the edges. You've been alone too long. It must be lonely here this time of year.'

'And freezing.'

'That's what I'm here for.' He put a hand out and began to stroke the side of her face. 'He's a pretty little snapper. I thought his Ma would be a looker. And there's something about him, something unreal, made me think there wasn't a proper Dad in the picture. Now, wasn't that a bit of luck for me?'

∾

THE SHELLS WERE LIKE ORNAMENTS girls would put in a neck-lace. The cart needed something real, something like Tewke had in his cart. Riff-raff. He looked up and down the beach but the sand was spotless as far as he could see. He'd better go and ask where to find some. He went back to the cottage and pushed open the door.

'Get out, you spying little brat!' his mother shouted.

Damian could only stare. Without her clothes, she looked peeled, like a soft fruit. Putting her clothes back on wouldn't make her into his proper mother again, any more than a banana would be a proper banana if you put the skin back on. His face closed, like those shellfish that have to be prised open with a chisel. 'You wait till my father gets here,' he said.

He ran back to the shore. He picked up the wooden horse and held it to his chest, stroking its rough curves. Then he flung it far out to sea. The horse bobbed as the waves rolled over playfully. They seemed to offer invitation. He would go into the sea after the horse. He would keep going until he came to where the mermaids were.

∾

'YOU HAVE TO LET IT GO. It's a sea horse now,' Tewke's voice crept up behind him.

Damian continued wading into the water. He licked sticky salt from his upper lip. He even tasted like the sea.

Tewke felt sorry for the kid – no old man and a hopeless mother, although a smasher. He wanted to make it up to him, put a bit of magic in his life, something the boy could hold on to in the bumpy years to come. 'Don't you want to hear the mermaids sing?' He spoke in that soft way he had. In spite of himself Damian turned around. Tewke reached into the baggy pocket of his jacket and took out his shell. It was large and glossy, speckled black and orange, curled up into itself like a small cat. 'There's more things in the world than you can ever know – so don't go thinking you know it all.'

'You shouldn't have touched my mother,' Damian shouted.

'You don't own your mother,' Tewke held out the shell.

'My father...!' Damian began.

'Mermaids only sing once a day, at sunset,' Tewke said. 'If you miss that, they're gone until tomorrow. If there's no sun they keep their traps shut.'

Damian came out of the water. He was very cold and couldn't stop shivering. He put his ear to the shell's porcelain-cool curves. He gazed at Tewke wide-eyed as the music burst upon his brain. It was a song, clear as clear, girls' voices singing. And then he let out a cry of rage. He put out his fist and knocked the shell out of Tewke's hand and ran past him to the cottage.

'Poor little blighter,' Tewke shook his head. He slipped the earpiece of his Walkman out from under his thumb and picked up the shell. 'Who ever heard of a kid that didn't like the Spice Girls?'

∾

CONCERTO
GROSSMAN

Frederic Raphael

I HAVE ALWAYS ENVIED MUSICIANS. What could be more vir-
tuously self-serving than to sing for one's supper? Alas, not
even when allotted the triangle in my prep school was I ever
able to strike the right note at the right time; at Charterhouse,
I was definitely branded a 'non-singer' by the choirmaster. It is
bad enough to hear that all flesh is as grass without being ban-
ished forever from the number of those who can be trusted to
announce it in tune. To one beyond its magic scope, to be a
musician is not only an accomplishment, it is to have the entrée
to a hermetic and harmonious community. Who would argue
with Peter-Paul Grossman when he said, in a recent interview,
that he wished that half the time that he had devoted to the
cinema had been dedicated to Wagner or to 'the dance'.

Peter-Paul did not disclose exactly what he should have done
with the *other* half of his misused time; he left it hazily clear that
it was something of even greater cultural significance than
taking yet another dip with the Rhinemaidens. It is typical of
his determination at all times to renew himself that Peter-Paul
chose implicitly to discount the merits of his 1963 Freudian
version of *Winnie The Pooh* in which the brilliantly re-thought
Eeyore was said to be closely modelled on certain newly discov-
ered material on Karl-Gustav Jung. The fact that the imported
actor spoke partly in Schweizer-Deutsch irritated some Milne

scholars, but I agree that it created a marvellous perspective through incongruity.

It was that seminal 'Winnie Ze Poo', and its explosive critical reception, that convinced Gino Amadei, and Gino who almost convinced me, that we should ask my already famous college friend to direct the script on which I had been working for the last six months. It was based on my own story and, in my pettish way, I was not flattered when Peter-Paul first said that he did not normally do commercial crap. Nor was I wholly placated when, after a persuasive lunch at the Trattoria, he relented, on condition that A PETER-PAUL GROSSMAN FILM appeared above the title. The casting of Rosemary Titchbourne as Lola was another non-negotiable demand. Peter-Paul told us that what he valued about 'Rosie' – as opposed to 'some putative star' – was that she could *sing*.

After the film was finished, Gino Amadei said, 'I'm sorry but I have to tell you one thing: the Rosemary Titchbourne has a voice we never hear and the most audible ankles I have ever seen.' For one reason or another, *The Love of Lola Gerassi* never received a general distribution. As Grossman said in a recent interview, England is a Philistine country in which tolerance is all too often only another name for laziness. Peter-Paul attributed the failure of the film to 'the basically banal *donnée* and, of course, the Bistro-style music'. He had, he said, wanted to create the soundtrack himself, but 'the producer's vulgar and venal considerations had, alas, prevailed'. However, as *auteur* he had the grace to allow that the blame had finally to be his. When Peter-Paul says *mea culpa*, it is the cue for everyone to redden guiltily.

The first time I ever saw him, he was wearing blue jeans, Moroccan slippers and a tented beige duffel coat with its hood

half-latched over masses of that often photographed, and carica-
tured, curly black hair. He was carrying his breakfast tray across
the third court of St John's College on a November morning.
His porridge was being kept warm by a lustreless tin lid on top
of which a much-flagged quarto volume lay legibly open. As he
walked, he was reading with intimidating intensity, his corrugated forehead lined like a manuscript page, ruled and ready
for crotchets. There must have been a morning frost, for as he
stepped from the paved to the cobbled part of the way to the
Bridge of Sighs, his leading foot suddenly went shooting away
and up into the raw air. He skittered backwards and forwards,
at once, with his tray and his book. Happening to be on the way
to the buttery for my own breakfast, I watched and listened,
with malicious anticipation, for the clattering comedown of a
man whose reputation, even at the beginning of his first year,
both promised eminence and prompted spite. Instead, he
hopped, tottered, lurched, blundered in a cascade of stagger-
ingly balanced improvisations. Not only did he not fall, not
only did he not lose so much as a single lump of his porridge,
but he also contrived *both to turn a page of his book and to
continue reading.* Was there ever a more manifest annunciation
of genius?

As recent studies have shown, my generation at Cambridge
was top-heavy with theatrical talent. In the 1950s, the difficulty lay less in finding a prodigy to direct undergraduate productions than in recruiting the troops on whom he might exercise
his generalship. Emulous contemporaries who could not hold a
candle to Peter-Paul were not always ready to carry a spear for
him. My modesty was my salvation; I enrolled to play ignoble
Romans and rhubarbing mechanicals in a number of early
Grossman successes. In his version of *Macbeth*, I doubled as

Malcolm and as a branch manager in Birnam Wood; he schooled me to add a neoteric note (not always spotted by the groundlings) to my interpretation of the part of Cinna the poet; as Osric, I spoke broad Devonshire in a sly, if slightly unintelligible, allusion to Sir Walter Raleigh who, Peter-Paul postulated, was almost certainly in Shakespeare's mind as the courtier's macaronic model.

90   After being promptly laurelled with a research fellowship to study Comparative Anthropophagy, it argued great courage when Peter-Paul quite suddenly renounced his academic career. Since he had been sponsored by men unaccustomed to having their favours set – let alone chucked – aside, Grossman's decision to go to Paris in order to become a *clown* struck some of his intellectual Godfathers as picayune, not to say blasphemous. He justified himself, at a meeting of the Apostolic circle to which he had been elected at a younger age than anyone since Bertie Russell, by declaring that it was not some Bohemian caprice which took him to Paris, but an out-of-the-blue opportunity to learn 'the rhetoric of silence' offered him by the great mimetic sage, Touvian, to whom even Marcel Marceau himself conceded the last wordless word. By leaping into a world of pure gesture, Peter-Paul hoped to come back through a door 'on the far side of speech' and gain a new insight into 'the pharmacopoeia of mundane signs'. The effect of this declaration was heightened, as perhaps I should have mentioned, by the red nose, white face, bald wig, orange braces and baggy pants in which he delivered it.

∞

SYLVIA AND I WERE LIVING in Paris when word came that Grossman was coming to study with the white-faced master of the *Cirque Muet*. We were shivering that winter in a couple of rented rooms in the working-class district of Crimée, while I wrote my first novel, but I heard that a fellow apostle, with money in furs, had lent Peter-Paul a cosy flat on the Ile de la Cité whence he pedalled to his class in the *Onziéme*. I sent him a card saying that we should be glad to hear from him if he were lonely. He must have been studying silence too diligently to be able to respond.

A mere week or two after his unobtrusive arrival in a city where he had announced he knew no one, I saw a full-page interview with Grossman in *L'Express*. Its subject was 'La Musique Totale et la Chose Sociale'. One phrase was particularly Delphic: 'Pour moi,' P.-P.G. was quoted as saying, 'la logique est surtout un cri d'alarme!' When Sylvia said, 'Logic is above all a cry of alarm? What's that supposed to mean?' I replied that I thought that I could give it a sense, but that we needed Peter-Paul for a definitive exegesis. We did not get him until towards the end of that freezing winter in Crimée, when Sylvia and I received an invitation to a *'soirée unique'*, directed by Peter-Paul Grossman, in which a critical history of the world was to be encapsulated, with an interval, in terms of music, mime and movement. If I was touched that Peter-Paul remembered us, I was petty enough to frown when I shook the envelope in vain for the tickets I assumed he had enclosed.

Sylvia and I sat very high up in the Salle André Breton, somewhere in the Marais, and were properly chastened as Peter-Paul's little troupe challenged any number of *idées reçues* with a vocabulary, as it were, consisting only of lengths of coloured rope, three beach balls, two window-cleaner's ladders, a bath-brush, a trampoline and a unicycle. Some people were so shaken by the iconoclastic acrobatics that they left early, but we stayed to tell Peter-Paul how amused we had been. All at once, his forehead took on immensely responsible corrugations. He looked like a frighteningly polyvalent Labrador who had been threatened with the Nobel Prize for Frivolity.

I chose to think of it as a mark of favour, though it may have been more loyalty, that he agreed to be free to dine with us after the show. It had, of course, taken it out of him. Was Sylvia a little tactless when she raised the question of what had he meant by saying that logic was a sign of alarm? He responded by opening his mouth in an inaudible shriek which, nevertheless, turned every head in the not inexpensive restaurant to which he had led us. He had, as it were, piped ultrasonically like a bat and transformed the whole room into his belfry. When Sylvia made a weary face, I had to admit that my friend had somehow succeeded in making me feel that my wife had failed to see the point. My mood was not lightened when Peter-Paul deferred to me, instantly, after I had gestured to the waiter for the bill. At the door, the *patron* thanked him thoroughly for the old francs I could ill afford to spend.

Despite and perhaps on account of our affinities, Peter-Paul and I have never become close friends. Over the years, our paths have crossed, but we were never true *compagnons de route*. It was something of a surprise, therefore, when I was contacted by young Giles Carpenter, the president-elect of the Cambridge Union, and asked whether I was free on a certain date in the autumn. The thing was, Giles explained they were having a debate about Music. When I muttered sincere excuses on the grounds of incompetence, the conniving young man explained that Peter-Paul wanted the word 'music' taken in a very wide sense, as signifying the domain of the Muses. I said 'Peter-Paul? As in Grossman?' 'Of course.' 'Ah,' I said, 'and what is the motion exactly?' My question was, of course, tantamount to acceptance. 'That Today Memory Has Too Many Children,' Giles said. 'He hopes you'll propose.'

Despite Sylvia's Cassandran warning, I fell for it. As I started to write my speech, I was surprised at the virulence with which my first draft was laced. Intent only on the composition of amiable barbs, I armed more warheads than I ever guessed my arsenal contained. Only now did I realise how angry I was at his perversion of *Lola Gerassi* or at his appropriation of its *auteurship*. I had not even forgotten that he never returned the hospitality we could ill afford at the Brasserie de l'Hôtel de Ville. Had I, in consequence or merely in addition, seriously disliked his setting of *Dido and Aeneas* in a Calcutta knocking shop and of *Ariadne auf Naxos* in the Betty Ford Institute? My vituperation stopped short of saying that he had claimed poetic licence without being a poet, authorship without ever having written a word, and a place in the pantheon only on the strength of being panned, but you could hear the squeal of its brakes.

Before the debate, there was a cheerful dinner, with heaps of mashed potato. When we lined up to go into the chamber, my opponent affected horror at the sheaf of paper which I revealed myself to be carrying. 'You've prepared,' he said, quite as if this were a breach of all civilised precedent, 'You bet,' I said.

Called to speak first, I was nervous, but I did not tremble. I got early laughs by pouring feline praise on Peter-Paul who, I said, was the very instance of the only child who made all his siblings redundant. His books, his paintings, his operatic productions, his stage happenings proved that the brother of the Muses had so upstaged his sisters that they would be well-advised to marry people who could find them jobs in subsidised theatres. There was a cry of 'ooh' at this below-the-belt reference to Rosie Titchbourne's frequent appearances in Peter-Paul's operatic productions. I sorted my papers quickly and proceeded to what I paraded as a sincere tribute to my opponent, who lay slumped on the bench opposite me in a style possibly owing something to Henry Moore's dying warrior. Willing to wound, but lacking the killer instinct, I ended by saying that I looked forward to hearing how many new art forms the great innovator had conceived during my defence of obsolete forms and old hats. However, I warned the audience not to be too easily seduced by my opponent as he played all the parts in his own Concerto Grossman. He was, I reminded them, a particular virtuoso on his own trumpet.

I sat down to solid applause. When Peter-Paul rose, it was, it seemed, in articulated instalments. He less walked than ramped, like some doomed but dignified caterpillar, to the despatch box. Once there, he groped in an inside pocket and produced a sheaf of paper. So much, I thought, for the sly fox's lack of preparation. He found a pair of glasses – age blights even a prodigy – and piled his script before him. He peered and saw that the sheets were blank. He sighed and turned them the other way up. To his clownish chagrin, he revealed them to be blank on both sides. My feeling of pity was supplanted by apprehension as the audience's rustle of embarrassment turned to a growl of amused complicity. They, and I, had realised that my paper bullets had not even scratched the man whose fire I was now fated to endure.

How shall I describe the fifteen minutes which followed? In front of my eyes, and with gesture alone, Peter-Paul composed cadenzas and improvised riffs in a speechless speech which denounced me as a commonplace novelist, a trudging cineaste, a commercial traveller, a diurnal and pedestrian reviewer, an uxorious husband and a decidedly overrated tennis player. As for Music, what part had I ever played in its inner counsels? I had, he indicated, after tuning an invisible instrument which still failed to utter a tolerable note, never been better than a futile second fiddle. He had, it seemed, observed me for years and seen nothing he did not despise. My speech had suggested that he had usurped a dominant place in the arts without being an artist. I was now proved to be wrong: his art was that of an assassin; the Concerto Grossman, which I had dared him to compose, was his silent and lethal equaliser.

95

LIKE A CIRCLE IN A SPIRAL

Russell Hoban

∞∞∞

T HE PAST DOESN'T GO AWAY; anybody with regrets knows 97
that: what you found and what you lost — it's all still
there in your head with the faces and the voices, the
music and the silence. Is it possible that it's outside your head
as well, like any other road you've travelled? And a song *can* take
you back to the past, can't it?

Her name was Lucinda, and the first time I ever saw her was
on the Embankment near the Albert Bridge. I used to go jog-
ging every morning back then: down Beaufort Street to the
Embankment, then on past the bridge as far as Swan Walk
where I turned around. Close by the bridge was a bronze nude
— I called her Monica — whose standing figure was so chaste and
unflaunting that I always slapped her bottom as I passed. It's
not a liberty I'd take now but things were more free and easy
in 1970.

This particular October morning was a foggy one: people
appeared out of a whiteness and disappeared back into it. The
sounds from the river were muted and mysterious. Monica was
wet and glistening, cold to the touch. There was no one else near
her on the out trip but on the return there was this young
woman leaning against the balustrade with her back to the
river: long honey-coloured hair, a Pre-Raphaelite face, and a
willowy figure, tall and graceful in faded blue jeans, a baggy

mauve jumper, and brown cowboy boots that looked hard-travelled. She was quite still but she looked as if she might in the next moment be somewhere else. Her beauty in the fog was so sudden, so startling that I stopped in my tracks just as my right hand made contact with Monica's left buttock. '"Round",' said the young woman.

'That's how God meant them to be,' I said.

'"Like a circle in a spiral",' she sang, '"like a wheel within a wheel".' Her voice was breathy and intimate but with a lot of distance and it gave me goosepimples. 'Round' was the first word of 'The Windmills of Your Mind' and I'd been singing that song as I jogged.

'"Never ending or beginning...",' I continued.

'"Never ending or beginning...".' She said it with a slow smile and that was the beginning of us; we disappeared into the fog and within a week she'd moved in with me. She had no bags, no boxes, nothing but the clothes she stood up in. She didn't want to go back for anything, she said; there were difficulties she preferred not to talk about.

She seemed to be the woman I'd been looking for all my life but couldn't have predicted; there was a strangeness about her, a wildness that fascinated me: I was never sure what she'd say or do next. I could scarcely believe that I'd found her, that she loved me, that she was mine: every time I drifted off to sleep with her beside me I wondered if she'd be there when I woke up.

Her fragrance was partly patchouli, partly herself. There was often a smell of incense as well; they sold it at Forbidden Fruit, the shop on the corner where I bought clothes for her that first week – boots and a cloak and embroidered things from Afghanistan and Tibet. Other shopping trips resulted in a floaty blue shift with gold stars and a purple velvet suit with knee breeches. She was delightful in whatever she wore.

And our breakfasts: I was so proud to be seen with her at a time of morning that told the world we'd spent the night together! Sometimes we went to Asterix in the King's Road; sometimes we bought croissants at a bakery in the Fulham Road. I used to buy coffee beans at Moore Brothers in the Fulham Road, then I ground them in a Moulinex and brewed them in a cafetière, like Michael Caine in *The Ipcress File*. It was a proper coffee ceremony, with the smell of the freshly ground beans certifying the intimacy of the hour.

I'd been working on a novel called *Here and Now* and not making much headway, but, with Lucinda around, the pages began to move forward. While I put in regular hours at my desk she was in and out on some project of her own, but she wouldn't tell me what it was. She'd saved up enough money from temping, she said, to buy herself some time. All in all, life was good; everything seemed more so: the buses were deliciously red and the lights were very bright.

We were often on Hungerford Bridge; the simple act of crossing the water to the South Bank became more than itself and magical with the lights on the water, the boats coming and going under the night sky, and all around us the brilliant panorama of domes and spires and illuminated clocks that recorded the moments that were passing. We listened to all kinds of music together; we went to the South Bank for Dietrich Fischer-Dieskau and *Die schöne Müllerin*, for *Die Schöpfung* and the Bach B minor Mass, to the Albert Hall for Ravi Shankar, and to the Borshtch 'n' Tears in Beauchamp Place for supper and Russian songs performed live. When I listen to *Die Schöpfung* now I start crying at the point where it bursts into light with 'und es ward Licht', but I can't do the orchestra and the singers properly in my head, so that music isn't with me as much as some popular songs are.

Lucinda was very interested in songs, always listening attentively to any that were new to her and wanting to know what year or at least what decade the old ones were from. Our record collection ranged from Monteverdi through Leadbelly to Bartók and Ziggy Stardust, but the song that was inseparable from that time was 'The Windmills of Your Mind'. Lucinda used to sing it in the kitchen and in the bath and she sometimes hummed it quietly during our evening walks. We had a single of it, with a vocal by Noel Harrison. That record is gone, along with everything else that ended on the day when Lucinda stopped being there. *Here and Now* never did get finished.

Time doesn't heal anything; on the afternoon of the 27th of November 1997, which was the twenty-seventh anniversary of the day she stopped being there, I couldn't get 'The Windmills of Your Mind' out of my head. I wanted to see Lucinda's face but I had no photographs. Recalling a Burne-Jones princess who looked like her, I climbed on to a chair to get *Pre-Raphaelite Women* from an upper shelf. The song had got to 'Like a tunnel that you follow to a tunnel of its own' when one of the chair legs gave way and I crashed to the floor, hitting the back of my head on the mini hi-fi on my desk as I fell.

There was some blood but the wound wasn't deep. What surprised me was the change in my vision: it was suddenly sharper, with more detail and more vivid colours than before. I smelled patchouli and found myself looking up from Lucinda's bare feet to the rest of her in a flowered kimono. She was continuing the song: '"down a hollow to a cavern where the sun has never shone…"'

'Lucinda!' I said.

'What?' she said.

'You're here!'

She gave me one of her slow smiles. 'I live here.'

'I'm having a little attack of confusion,' I said. I ran my hand up her leg; it was moist from the bath, warm and solid and as shapely as ever.

'You don't seem confused,' she said.

'Indulge me. What year is this?'

'Nineteen seventy. You want to be indulged right there on the floor?'

I felt around behind me, then sat up. No desk, no mini hi-fi. The room was different; we were in the flat in Mulberry Close in Beaufort Street where we'd lived in 1970. I got up and went to a window. In the garden of the convent next door the nuns were playing ball. 'O God,' I said, 'is it going to happen again?'

'Not if you don't want it to. I wish you'd make your mind up.'

'But you're not a day older. This can't be real.'

'Of course it can: reality is all kinds of things at all kinds of times. Sometimes it's "Like a door that keeps revolving in a half-forgotten dream or the ripples from…"'

'"A pebble someone tosses in a stream…",' I sang in a whisper, feeling as young as I'd been when we met but Lucinda's voice had faded; she was gone and Mulberry Close was gone. I was alone again, back where I'd been before the chair leg gave way. I put my hand to my head which was still bleeding. 'I wish you were a little less volatile, Lucinda,' I said to the emptiness she'd left behind. Obviously the whole thing had been a hallucination.

I've got several books on the human brain, but I couldn't remember what was back there where the mini hi-fi had dented my skull. Was it the limbic system? I liked the sound of that but I didn't want to look it up, I was afraid that if I lost my innocent ignorance I might lose this strange new ability to hallucinate Lucinda and 1970. I'd loved her so much! If I went back to 1970 and kept going back there, would we simply work our way forward to the bad part again? Even if it wasn't real I didn't want that. Although I wasn't as certain about reality as I used to be. Lucinda had always derided my insistence that it should be the same every day. 'Reality is like the weather,' she said: 'it changes from moment to moment.'

On the other hand, maybe I wasn't the one who was going back: I'd sung that song lots of times without reaching Lucinda and 1970. Maybe *she* was the one who was putting us both back in that time and place. With her limbic system or whatever, from wherever she was now. Maybe *she* was hallucinating *me*. Or was she a sort of ghost, the residual energy of herself imprinted on me and accessible in moments when my mind was jolted out of its usual tracks?

Thinking about it was a waste of time; I knew in my heart that I wanted to be with her again at any cost. So I sat on the floor where I'd fallen when the chair collapsed, shut my eyes, and began the song again. Nothing happened until I reached 'Like a clock whose hands are sweeping past the minutes of its face.' Then I smelled patchouli as her voice came in with '"And the world is like an apple whirling silently in space..."'.

With my eyes still shut I found her naked left foot again. Such a marvellous magical foot, like a handle to happiness, still moist and warm from the bath. I opened my eyes and there she was in the flowered kimono. 'Oh, Lucinda!' I said, 'Lucinda, Lucinda, Lucinda!'

'What?' she said.

'You're here!'

'I live here,' she said with that slow smile. 'We've done this already, just a few moments ago. I'm Lucinda, you're Phillip; this is 1970.'

As before, I looked around: we were once more in Mulberry Close. Again I went to the window and saw the nuns playing ball in their garden. The last of the afternoon sunlight gilded the roof of the convent with such a goodbye look that I almost wept. My desk was in a different place and my old manual type-writer was on it; the computer and printer were gone. There was a record player with two speakers but no mini hi-fi and no CDs. There was a TV but no video recorder. There were only a few bookshelves and no videotapes.

'So here we are in 1970,' I said.

'That's what they're calling it,' said Lucinda.

I wasn't feeling twenty-seven years younger. 'How do I look?' I said.

'You need a shave one day more than yesterday, otherwise the same.'

'I have to tell you, Lucinda: either I'm not here or you're not here — one or the other.'

'I know how it is with you when you're working,' she said: 'everything else goes away.'

'That isn't what I'm talking about: where I am is 1997 and this isn't really happening.'

'Let me show you,' she said, 'what's really happening.' She shrugged out of the kimono and it slithered to her feet.

∞

WELL, AS LUCINDA SAID, reality is all kinds of things at all kinds of times. Or perhaps you might say that it's negotiable, like a plea bargain in a court of law: you settle for the best deal you can get.

The flat had filled with twilight. As we lay there smoking I was looking forward to some leisurely drinking and a quiet evening at home, but Lucinda reminded me that we were going out. 'We've got tickets for *The Tea Party* and *The Basement*.'

'Pinter?'

'Right.'

'We've already seen those plays, haven't we?'

'No, we haven't. It'll do you good to get away from your desk for a while.'

'I *have* been away from my desk for a while. Remember?'

'I'm talking culture,' she said.

So we did culture. It wasn't too bad because, although I'd already seen *The Tea Party* and *The Basement* the first time around with 1970 I'd forgotten them entirely. We had a late supper at Le Bistingo in the King's Road and when we got back to Beaufort Street we still had the intimacy of the small hours ahead of us. I'm not talking about sex now, but the miracle of getting through the night with her beside me again. What a long desert those twenty-seven years had been! What about tomorrow morning? I wondered. What year will it be? Nineteen ninety-seven had offered me nothing as good as this.

Tomorrow morning was Sunday, still 1970. We slept in, then went out for pancakes at Asterix. While eating what was on my plate I consumed Lucinda with my eyes, afraid she might disappear at any moment. When we got back to the flat we grazed on the Sunday papers for a while, then I sat down at the typewriter. The unfinished pages of *Here and Now* were stacked next to it but I couldn't bear to look at them so I typed a title, 'Like a Circle in a Spiral' and began to write this. Confusing, certainly, but the best deal I could get. As the afternoon sunlight waned I went to the window and saw that the nuns were

still playing ball in their garden. Lucinda was sitting with the
Sunday Times Magazine in her lap. Her eyes were closed and she
was singing, very softly, 'My One and Only Love': "'The very
thought of you makes my heart sing like an April breeze on the
wings of spring…'"

I left the desk and kissed her. 'Me too,' I said.

She opened her eyes. 'You too what?'

'What you were singing.'

'Oh,' she said.

It stayed 1970 that day and night and it kept on being 1970.
As one day followed another we did again the things we did the
first time around: we went to the South Bank for Fischer-
Dieskau and the Schubert, for the Haydn and the Bach as
before, to the Albert Hall and our other venues. Can it go on
like this indefinitely? I wondered. Or will there be an end to it?

It did not go on indefinitely. One morning Lucinda got out
of bed singing 'My One and Only Love' and suddenly wasn't
there; she simply vanished before my eyes exactly as she'd done
the first time, and with the very same song. I'm not sure how
long ago her second going was; the dates on the newspapers only
go to 31 December 1970, then they start over again on 27
November.

The nuns are still playing ball. When I finish this story I'll
just have to write it again because that's the reality of my 1970.
I wonder what year Lucinda's in now and who her one and only
love is. I wonder how it was for him when she was with me. I
wonder when it'll be my turn again.

∞

THE YELLOW-HAIRED BOY

Michèle Roberts

S OMETIMES HE CRIED HIMSELF TO SLEEP. Mostly he just felt a dull despair like a stomach ache. He was a failure. Everybody told him so, in gestures, in looks. They stuck out their lips at him and grimaced, or they shrugged when he walked by. When the important talents were handed out, the musical ones, he got none. His two older brothers could not only recite poems but play the whistle and the pipes and the drum. At their mother's funeral they soothed everybody's hurt by producing melodies which wrapped themselves round you like harsh coats, keeping you warm but scratching you at the same time. He, the third brother, the yellow-haired boy, hovered on the edges of the crowd, glowering and looking away as the coffin woven of willow was lowered into the shallow grave. Afterwards, at the wake, he stood near the doorway, so that he could escape if need be, and listened as his two brothers sang the customary lament and enchanted all the villagers with their sweet voices chasing each other in the air like swallows, making anguish a beautiful thing so that soon enough everyone was in tears. Except for him, scowling at his feet and unable to look anybody in the eye.

He was born in the north of the country, near the sea, on the east coast. Everybody in the village was poor, which gave them a certain equality, but between themselves they acknowledged important differences. So and so could make the best bread or plough the fastest, or lift the heaviest weights. The talent they revered most highly was that for making music and singing. Their form of riches, the only one they had. They worked all day, seven days a week, to wrestle themselves a living, grubbing subsistence from the soil. There was never anything to spare, for they had to give generously to the nuns and monks, their landlords, who lived in the great double monastery which hung above the village like a thundercloud, but nonetheless they found ways of enjoying themselves whenever they could. In winter especially, in the long dark evenings, they entertained themselves with their home-made music. Officially, they were all Christians now, but at night, when the nuns and monks were asleep, and the priest kept to his own house, they went back to the songs they knew best, that had been handed down to them generation from generation, long before the Christians arrived and converted them.

Music surrounded the yellow-haired boy all through his childhood. People sang as they worked, to encourage themselves, to sweeten their hardships, to stave off tedium. Men's and women's voices reached for each other according to the rhythms of their labour, the steady beat of arms lifting implements, bodies that bent and stretched and stooped over the earth. After supper, round the fire, they sang other songs that told stories of gods and heroes and spirits, songs that leaned steadily into the night and held off the darkness outside, songs that were only interrupted when the singer finally gave in to fatigue and tumbled asleep, the verse to be taken up and continued by the next person who knew the words. The pauses and repetitions and yawns became part of the song, woven into its fabric, enriching it. They began learning music as soon as they drew their first breath. Mothers sang to their tiny babies as they fed them and scolded them and hushed them, as they carried them on their backs into the fields. There were songs for giving birth, for transferring courage and strength to the labouring woman, songs of praise and thanks when the baby was born. There were songs for listing the skills of a lover and songs for lamenting when a lover left. There were sung charms against accidents and disease and plenty of songs for death, when the departing soul was sped on its way in collective harmonious grief. It was normal to sing, it was ordinary and good, like working and eating and weeping and making love.

Life was hard, and it was simple. The year wheeled and spun through the seasons and the people celebrated the important moments of planting and harvesting with festivals when they sang and danced and played music. They killed one of their precious animals and ate meat, on these special occasions, not just the usual barley porridge, and told stories and poured quantities of wine and beer down their throats, and then they passed round the harp and sang, each person in turn. Outside the sea whipped itself up, and the wind howled, and lashed the trees, and darkness prowled round the house like a hungry beast, and the rain drummed on the thatch, but inside, huddled around the smoky fire, they felt safe for the moment, and replete, and they rejoiced by singing. Everyone could sing, except for him, the peculiar yellow-haired boy. He just wouldn't try. He wouldn't join in. He rejected them and their merrymaking and sulked in a corner. He could not be coaxed or persuaded.

During his childhood, while his mother was still alive, various attempts had been made to teach him to sing, since it did not seem to come naturally. His two brothers leaned on their mother's knees, and sang to her, and she waved to the yellow-haired boy to listen to them and copy them, but he would not. He flung out of the house, and she sighed in bewilderment and exasperation. On another occasion his father held his mother's hand and sang a duet with her, and they smiled at the yellow-haired boy with their eyes and invited him to join in with them, but he would not. He turned away and stared at the floor and they felt hurt by his refusal and could not understand it. One by one they gave up trying to teach him better. The priest had no more success. When he sat the village children in a row on a wooden bench at the front of the tiny church and taught them to sing Christian songs and psalms, they duly squeaked and growled their way through this new music while the priest beat his fist against his palm and bawled out the notes one step ahead. Over and over he made them sing until they were hoarse. Only the yellow-haired boy did not join in. Blushing and stammering, he stared at his feet when sarcastically invited to explain why he could not behave like the others, have a go, do his best, offer his mite, all for the glory of Almighty God. They all sniggered at him, the rest of the choir, his erstwhile companions, and the priest fetched him a slap and bundled him out of the church. Eventually, his parents gave up. They accepted he would not come to much, and set him to work minding the cows. Then his mother died, and he could not join in mourning her because he could not sing. He had lost her, and he had lost his name too. Nobody used it any more. They addressed him as daftie, or old croaker, or frog in my throat.

He turned out to be no good at minding the cows because he could not sing the cattle call to fetch the animals in. Most jobs required some ability with singing. It was, after all, the way things got done. Finally they set him to the only task they could think of which did not require some capacity for music. He became the one who cleaned out the cattle sheds and the stables, forking up the hot manure and then spreading clean straw under the beasts in their stalls. He liked the job, because the animals did not laugh at him, and responded to a pat or stroke, or a whisper.

He still had to go indoors to eat, however, to be reminded, every time he went to collect his bowl of food, of his deficiencies, when the others called him names, or tripped him up so that he sent his soup flying, or secretly gripped the skin of his forearm and twisted it till he screamed and they praised him for his fine singing voice.

He developed the habit of grabbing his dish of supper and retiring with it back to the barn, where he gobbled it listening to the munching of the cows. They didn't mind him. They left him in peace and tolerated him. He slept in the stable whenever he could, to be out of the way of the other boys and young men, who all bedded down together in the house in front of the dying fire and whose idea of fun was to thrust a glowing ember against his mouth as he slept. So he grew up. He glowered and looked rough and people kept away from him. They tut-tutted about how difficult he was, about the weight of the chip on his shoulder, about how he couldn't take a joke. Girls did not come near him, for they had been warned that he was liable to fly into violent rages and attack people. His two brothers, being so talented at singing, were both put, as soon as they reached a suitable age, into the great monastery above the town, and so he never got a chance to know them properly nor they he. They had not felt able to stick up for him or to help him, because they had their own survival to worry about, and so their departure to the monastery left him indifferent and uncaring. His father remarried and started a new family. The yellow-haired boy fended for himself.

THE HARVEST FESTIVAL CAME ROUND. A great feast was prepared, of roast fish, chicken and ducks, porridge was boiled up in quantities, jugs of beer were set in readiness. The yellow-haired boy grabbed his share and ran away with it behind the screen which stood between the door and the fire to keep out the draughts. He ate with his head down, one arm curved protectively around his bowl, his eyes swerving from side to side to check for possible marauders who might steal his food. Then the food was cleared away and just the drink left, and the harps, pipes, whistles and drums were brought out, and people started playing and singing. Round the circle went the instruments, and one by one, in turn, each person sang a song. They sang with such courage and nobility, he thought, in the middle of their lives so threatened by poverty or starvation or sudden death, they made music out of that, they stared death in the face, in the teeth of death they brought forth sounds of astonishing sweetness and strength, they tossed down their beer and shouted, they danced, they sank back down on the benches and listened to more singing. And he cowered in the shadows and envied them. When they remembered him, and dragged him out from his hiding-place, and mockingly thrust a harp into his hands and commanded him to sing, he flung the harp into their faces and blundered outside into the cowshed.

All his life he had sworn that he hated singing and loathed it, that it was a nonsense for old people and women, it had nothing to do with him and who he was. This was the best defence he had been able to find for himself, but on a night like this it got ripped to pieces and he was forced to know how much he cared that he was not like the others. On the clean straw he had put down earlier that day, he lay and cried. He wished he could dazzle the rest with his gifts, he longed to be the one who got the prize, who commanded praise, compliments, love. Snot and tears dripped down his face. He bawled into his hands, until he had cried himself out, and then he wiped his nose on his sleeve and lay back exhausted.

Now he felt curiously at peace. The drama of shame and humiliation was over. He was on his own, where no one could see him. He was as real as a nail in the door, as the rope slung from the rafter; no more and no less. He spread his hands wide and looked at them. He spoke out loud: 'I am empty; I have nothing; I am not the favourite; I was not my mother's favourite child and never can be now.' It was a comfort, somehow, to recognise that. It was the truth, that was all.

The darkness around him altered subtly. It shifted and glimmered. It seemed to be recomposing itself into a finer and softer blackness shot through with tiny lights, as though he were lying outside looking up at the stars. But he knew very well he was not. He could hear the cows munching noisily, the swish of their tails, the occasional stamp of their hooves. He could smell their straw and manure. He raised himself on one elbow and looked around. His back was tingling as though someone were stroking his spine. There was a point of light at the far end of the shed so he supposed that someone had entered with a lantern and was come in search of him. He shrank back against the heap of straw on which he lay, wishing that he could hide. It was too late. Through the glittering darkness came a stranger, walking in a shape of light that surrounded and travelled with him like a hooded cloak. He was a part of the darkness, he emerged from it and seemed made of it, and yet at the same time he radiated light. Lanternlight, starlight, moonlight, he seemed to bring them all with him into the close, dark cowshed.

He walked up to the yellow-haired boy and addressed him as

though he knew him. He called him by his name, which no one else ever used.

'Caedmon,' he said, 'sing to me.'

Caedmon struggled up to his knees. He gawped at his visitor.

'I can't,' he said, 'I can't sing. That was why I left the others indoors, and came out here. I'm useless at singing. I'm a failure.'

'Nonetheless,' the stranger insisted, 'you shall sing.'

His beautiful face was so kind that Caedmon felt like crying all over again, only this time with astonishment and joy.

'What shall I sing about?' Caedmon asked.

'Sing about creation,' returned the other, 'and about how creation begins.'

Caedmon scrambled to his feet and shut his eyes, and saw his mother's face. He saw her coffin, and he saw it being lowered into the ground. And so he began to sing. A voice got up inside him and poured out of him, strong, confident, golden. The words arrived at the same time as the notes, they twisted together to make this new music he had never heard before and which was shaping him, hollowing him out, like water roaring forth from a cavern underground, singing about his mother and how he had lost her and she would never come again, for these were the new times, when either she was gone for ever and utterly departed from him and he would never find her again, or else he would have to seek her, to find her anew in the world that was so full of such difficulty, such loss and such pain but such sweetness too, such music, such moments of harmony. The stranger, the man who was dark and glittering, golden and black, stood close to Caedmon. He attended, quite still, until Caedmon had finished. Then he vanished. The light went out and the cowshed was pitch dark once more. Caedmon stumbled out, across the yard. He approached the house, slowly and tentatively, and went inside, to join the others there.

With thanks to Bede's *Ecclesiastical History of the English Nation.*

THEORY
AND PRACTICE

Candia McWilliam

'I LIKE BEING COLD when I'm working,' said James. 'It stops 117 my brain taking off its shoes.'

'Then you must be happy in your work,' said Anna, who was new and knew only that he worked as a singer, but this was Scotland, so reliably chilly. Anyhow, she wasn't concentrating more than she need, since across the cafe where they sat was a couple she could not stop staring at. They had the look of people to whom good things happen, without effort. He – it was a he and a she, as conventional as that, though he was younger than she – he was putting sugar into her coffee with the precision and attention of someone either well rehearsed or highly evolved.

'Will you take sugar?' asked James, annoying her by his observation.

'No,' she said in a voice unnecessarily unpleasant. And she watched James to see if he were watching the sugared woman, whose profile might have been cut clean from paper and whose blouse was white at the neck and wrists of her velvet coat. Not that Anna minded where James in particular looked. But she knew that the woman with the sugared coffee had been built up layer over painted layer by the admiring glances of others.

'I don't take sugar except in emergencies or after shock,' Anna said to James. She ran her heel under the table along the edge of the violin case that lay on the floor. It felt small, but reassuring.

With the coffee came a complementary biscuit in waxed paper. She passed hers to James and hoped that he would not take this too kindly. She supposed not. It was her belief that singers, as opposed to instrumentalists, noticed very little that distracted from the plot. Singers reacted, commented, fed, fornicated, wept, forgot, and woke up fresh and ready to do it all again. Instrumentalists observed, vibrated, annotated, remembered, broke their hearts, and sank into reflection and nostalgia.

Singers sang out loud in the street and walked on air and threw roses at their spurned lovers. Instrumentalists were not thus mad but in their own way sad, full of lost notes and tunes almost-heard. Violinists were the worst, except maybe for the odd timpanist; always hearing different shadings of silence, of sound about to arrive.

The music around Anna and James, just at present, was that of Blondie; sounds like a celestial car crash, with Debbie Harry's girly voice commenting over the metal sounds like a blue light over a wet road.

James, as she'd expected, ate the two biscuits without missing a beat. The incuriosity of singers, their failure to enquire!

'Why are you always so furious?' asked James.

So she was found out, and so she fell in love.

When it began, they had known one another for the lifespan of two operas, but not of course well, since she had always been in the pit among the other violins in the orchestra, and he in the chorus among the other male voices, *his* instrument.

For Anna's theory had foundered. James sang, but he had the sensibilities she had ascribed to instrumentalists. Because she was pig-headed and enjoyed classifying people, she twisted experience to fit theory. James was the first singer she had known who did not whip his voice out and use it at inappropriate times. He kept quiet about it. It was a large, deep voice. His was an intelligent, but not a dandified, diction. Jane had never once heard him break into spontaneous song; whereas, she knew, there were times she had been so happy, so touched – these times with James especially – that, had her violin been a part of her, growing between her fingers, she would have bent to her music like a spinner to her wheel. And spun it out   119 of herself.

The company toured the country, slowing down a little in the winter as the snow closed the smaller roads up into the Highlands, and the ferries out over to the islands were occasionally cancelled under storm. Then the forty of them might give a surprise performance in some town where there'd not often been an opera. Not something you could say for that many places, though, in a country so riddled with music as this: where an inch of air had five lines to it, every drink took you closer to a song and there had been a *Makropulos Case* in Ballachulish.

∾

HERE THEY WERE, IN A GUEST HOUSE waiting for the wind to fall so they could get over and perform a whittled-down *Rosenkavalier* at the head of the loch – in a house to be reached by lorry along the ruined road or by dinghy over the loch.

'Not as bad as that *Macbeth* on the diddy wee island with the quarry on it,' said Gregor, who drove their props lorry. 'And nothing to the place under the flightpath of those fighters – burst out the ground like murder and crack your ears out yer heid.'

The lounge of the guest house was not warmed by the electric fire that showed its two red bars in the gloom. A mirror reflected only cream paint and deep red cloth in its spotted depths. Although the room was not warm, it smelt of things that had been; meat, old coffee, skin, dogs, wool. It was the time of late afternoon when the bare shapes of trees seem about to make sense, when the cries of rooks, desolate by day, are becoming comforting so long as you are not alone with them.

Members of the orchestra and the chorus were billeted all around, some with farmers, some at bed and breakfasts, most here at the Little White Rose guest house. The soloists were ensconced with a man who farmed fish and knew the double-bass player. It was a bit down a glen in a house with tapestries that were cruel to the voice, so that the Marschallin had cried off just now, and was here in the bitter lounge with its overlay of smells that might do better if heated through.

Her name was Verena and her dilemma was the old one, to which she gave much poignancy in this part. It was coming to be time to believe her mirror and not the voices of the ever younger young men who sought and then pained her. She did not apply an understanding of her art to her life; although, the other way about, the connection beat for all to see.

Anna had learned to view Verena with some gentleness. Not to blame her for the insistence of others upon her beauty, her fragility, her closeness to imbalance. Anna could see by now that Verena was a woman with yellow hair and a profile that in this teatime gloaming cut itself clear of her plain white blouse. A woman who wanted peace, to settle down, and to rid her lungs of dust fallen on her from tapestries depicting women who looked much as she did, – but bent over stitched green waters under stitched blue trees, always in sight of cold, beautiful young men and tight-waisted dogs with hard collars and crossed paws, resting resigned under long noses.

Among these tapestries, that hung from steel bars tipped like lances, the soloists had eaten off pewter, dressed in all their clothes to protect them from the cold that struck up from the floor. The fish they ate had not been the farmed silver crop of the house, but sardines, from their tins, that lay along the table, browsed by the several cats whose soft grey fur lent the room – forty feet high – any comfort it had.

'Will you take the lorry – Anna, Verena – or the dinghy?' Gregor asked, blowing across a can of Stella and listening like an oboist. 'The lorry'd be safer.'

'The boat,' the two women said.

'Should you?' James asked Verena, displaying manners. And quickly, so that it should not seem a consideration of age but of health, he added, 'with your cough?'

'It'll clear it up,' said Verena. 'It'll blow me through.'

They had half an hour to get ready. The bath ran brown but hot and Anna put on her thermals and her black velvet gown in the attic room with a feeling almost of a party to come. James washed in her bath after she had stepped out of it. He admired the marks the peaty water had made upon Anna's pink skin as she dried herself.

It was a Scots bathroom, explicitly connected to all the other bathrooms of the guesthouse, its hard floor and bare pipes conveying the human rush of talk, the punctuating declarations of water arriving and departing.

James wiped a place in the watery mirror to shave and spied on Anna through the cleared patch of mirror. 'I love you,' he told her, and again, after they had covered their evening clothes with waterproof gear and put their feet into seaboots.

Their shoes were to go overland in the lorry, with the most part of the company and the silver rose itself, almost the only prop they were to take. They were to perform in a chamber equipped with its own great bed, in which Verena would be able, in some comfort, to lament the agonising failure of her dazzle.

Outside the sky was purely deep blue. James walked holding Verena by the arm and Anna by the hand. She had a hole in her glove and could feel where her skin touched his, the sort of thing she did not believe in. The stars being higher in Scotland, the group of them craned as they walked down to the waterside and along the trembling wooden jetty, where the boat was tied up.

In it were three rows of wooden benches, and in its stern sat a man leaning relaxed on the tiller of the outboard. The light at the end of the jetty was flat like a white cymbal, blaring out brassy light. It was sealoch: tidal, choppy, edged with shingle on whose tough-grassed rim sat a group of unbelieving sheep, passing low comment as they saw the woollen boat load assemble.

The ladder down into the dinghy trembled and blistered in the gloved hand. It felt as though it would snap if it felt you doubted it. The air seemed thinner, the stars higher and brighter, when they were out on the water.

The man in the stern had shaken hands with each of them as they arrived. His name was David.

He started the engine, listened to it like a man tuning up, waited till the note he wanted swelled and hit, and pointed the bow of the boat out towards a pale light.

'Whisky?' asked David, pulling a bottle from within his coat. Verena and James yes. All the singers yes. The voice can maybe take it when the fingers cannot. At any rate, Anna did not.

She watched James pass the bottle to Verena and wipe it first. She saw Verena wipe it again, as though absent-mindedly. She wondered how it might be to live without certainty, to be blown about by one's beauty, as Verena had been. Not to be safe, as she, Anna, was.

'Don't you mind?' asked another violin. Anna heard but she did not take it to heart. Perhaps she was becoming a singer. No longer capable of spoiling true notes by over-attention, of listening a thing to extinction.

123

James moved gingerly, keeping the dinghy trimmed, from the bow where the white prow of Verena's tragic face led them on to the night to come – at the head of the loch. He moved towards Anna, where she sat watching at the edge of the little boat. She smelled the whisky.

'I love the cold for work,' he said. 'This is just my sort of cold.'

Leaning her head against him just as she leant her head in to her instrument, she heard before it came, felt before she heard, the beginnings of his voice emerging not into words spoken, but into song, set off by the flying cold about them as they moved through its heart-subduing melody. He sang not from opera – that had brought together this group of people on water between mountains in a frail boat, that had made of himself and Anna a pair – but from something English, ecclesiastical, stiff, ponderous, apposite to the darkness and the imminent light.

'Proficiscere, anima Christiana, de hoc mundo! Go forth upon thy journey, Christian soul! Go from this world! Go, in the name of God the Omnipotent Father, who created thee! Go, in the name of Jesus Christ, our Lord, son of the living God, who bled for thee! Go, in the name of the Holy Spirit, who hath been poured out on thee!'

When James had completed the Priest's valediction to the

Soul of Gerontius, he did not have that look of repletion and infantile greed that Anna had often seen on the faces of singers. It was as though that big fluctuating account of travail and arrival had not come solely from him, but from all of them. And, as they disembarked at the other end of the water, it was into a world of light and released sweetness – as though time were for that night suspended by art in one cold house after a short journey.

∞

THE
OVER-RIDE

Rose Tremain

WHEN STEFAN MOUTIER WAS A CHILD, he was forbidden by his mother to sit on the stairs.

Madame Moutier was the concièrge of an expensive building in the 8th Arrondissement of Paris and she would remind her son: 'The stairs are not ours. They are the residents' territory and you shouldn't be there.'

But Stefan had noticed other things on the stairs which looked as if they shouldn't have been there: cats sleeping; bags of garbage left out. And so he disobeyed his mother. He decided to become as silent as a cat, as shapeless as a bag of garbage. That way, the residents would walk right by him and not notice him.

The most famous residents of the building were Guido and Claudette Albi. Madame Moutier boasted about them to the concièrges of other buildings in the area: 'The Albis, you know, the world-famous musicians.' But these other concièrges often said: 'Yes, Madame Moutier. But beware. Artistes are trouble. In the end, trouble will come.'

But trouble did not come for a long time. What came, all through Stefan Moutier's childhood and adolescence, was music. And this was why he sat crouched on the stairs. He was listening to the tides of Mozart and Haydn, of Brahms and Bruch, of Beethoven and Schubert, of Debussy and Ravel that came flooding out of the Albis' apartment. And when he grew up, married his childhood sweetheart, Monique, and left the building, he missed the Albis' music. In the night, while Monique slept beside him, he would often remember it and think, the staircase to the fifth floor was a brilliant place to be.

It wasn't that he was musically talented himself. He had no aspirations to be good at anything like that, and what he wanted from life, apart from Monique, he wasn't really able to say.

128   He went to work for the national gas company. He trained as a gas fitter and began to earn the kind of salary people told him was 'decent'. He considered himself fortunate.

He liked the fact that he wore overalls to work. This meant that he could save his own clothes for Sundays, when he and Monique would go and have lunch with Madame Moutier. He was a dark, good-looking young man and he enjoyed looking smart.

Often, during those Sunday lunches, he would ask his mother if the Albis were home and felt comfortable when she said they were. Frequently, however, the Albis were in New York or Chicago or Salzburg or Adelaide. Stefan would remember all the times he'd stowed their tan and green luggage into the boot of the chauffeured car and the way Guido Albi would put a scrunched-up piece of blue paper into his palm – a fifty franc note. But in all the years he'd sat on the stairs, the Albis had never seen him there. They didn't know he'd ever heard them play a single note.

∾

TROUBLE CAME TO STEFAN MOUTIER before it came to the Albis. He and Monique were driving down the Avenue de Clichy late one Saturday night, when a garbage collection truck pulled out in front of them. Monique was thrown through the window of

Stefan's new Peugeot into the maw of the truck.

Stefan got out of the car and stood in the road. He thought he was elsewhere and dreaming. He thought he was going to wake up in his bed with Monique beside him, so he just stayed still, waiting for this to happen. But it didn't happen. And from that moment, when Monique's life was thrown away, Stefan was stuck in a nightmare from which there appeared to be no exit.

∾

THE NATIONAL GAS COMPANY were enlightened employers. They had to be because gas, after all, was a lethal product and a man who has seen his wife die in a garbage truck will need time to recover before he can be trusted with it again.

They gave Stefan Moutier a month's paid leave of absence. His colleagues held a whip-round for a large funeral tribute in the shape of an M and then they said to him: 'Stefan, nobody is capable of getting over something like this on his own. You have to have help.'

They started taking him to bars in the evenings and making sure he was well and truly drunk by the time they saw him home. He drank a variety of things: beer, pastis, vodka, cognac, whisky, rum. He admitted to Madame Moutier: 'I don't much like the taste of any of them, except the beer, but I like what they do to me: they let me escape from the nightmare for a few hours.'

'All right,' said Madame Moutier, 'but take care. Your father was a drinker and couldn't stop once he'd started. Don't get so dependent on it that you won't be able to quit.'

∾

WHEN THE MONTH WAS GONE, Stefan put on his overalls and returned to work.

The Area Manager took him aside on his first morning back.

'We hope you will be able to continue in this job, Stefan,' he said. 'But I must inform you we will be monitoring you. It's nothing personal. Just the safety measures we always apply in circumstances like these.'

Stefan wanted to say: 'There are no other "circumstances like these"! This is worse than anything ever experienced by anyone working for this company!' But he stayed silent. He didn't want to be kicked out of his job.

130   But then he found he couldn't *do* the job any more. His hands shook. His vision, which had always been sharp, became unreliable. One minute he would be working on a boiler component and the next he'd be staring at nothing – at a terrifying void in front of his eyes.

He tried to conceal these things. A shot of alcohol at midday seemed to steady him. But now fear had crept into his nightmare, a fear so profound there were days when Stefan had to call in sick because he just couldn't cope with the idea of work.

It was on one of these days, while he lay alone in his bed, that he switched on the radio and heard some music that he recognised. He couldn't name it. He thought it might have been by Schubert. All he knew was that it was one of the pieces he used to listen to on the stairs outside the Albis' apartment.

And it brought him almost instantly to a decision: he couldn't work as a gas fitter any more. He was too afraid of what he might do, the mistakes he might make. He would give in his notice to the gas company. He would leave the apartment he'd shared with Monique and which now seemed chilly and full of shadows, and return to his mother. And when the distortions of vision came, when the nightmare was at its darkest, he would pray that the Albis weren't away in New York or Adelaide, but there on the fifth floor, playing their music behind the closed apartment doors, and he would sit on the stairs and listen.

Madame Moutier said: 'It's all very well, Stefan, but what are you going to do with yourself all day?'

Stefan reminded his mother that there were a hundred small tasks he could usefully do in the building – from carrying down luggage, to changing light bulbs, to cleaning windows.

'All right,' she said, 'but I can't spare you much money. You'll have to rely on tips. And don't spend them on drink, or you'll have nothing.'

He *had* nothing. Nothing was exactly what he had. No life. No job. No steady state of belonging in the world. He was alive, that was all. He could get plastered and remember what it was to laugh at a stupid joke, to feel affection towards his old friends and towards a particular café or bar. But beyond this, he was as good as dead. Days and weeks and then months passed and they seemed to go on ahead of him, or at a different pace, or somewhere else, leaving him behind.

Only once in a while did he get the feeling that he was waiting for something more to happen.

∾

IT WAS DURING THIS TIME that Guido Albi fell in love with a young Japanese cellist called Jenni Chen.

From behind the door of the Albis' apartment now came the sound of Claudette Albi's hysterical crying and the breaking of crockery and glass.

'You see, Madame Moutier,' said the neighbourhood con- cièrges, 'disruption and trouble. Exactly as we predicted.'

And it was true: the whole building could hear the weeping of Claudette and the furious shouting of Guido. Not only the building. These noises could be heard right across the courtyard and by the optometrist on the opposite side of the street.

The fourth floor residents came down to the concièrge's rooms and declared: 'We can't sleep, Madame Moutier. Our lives are being totally disrupted. Just because they're famous doesn't give them license to disturb the whole of the 8th Arrondissement.'

'I agree,' said Madame Moutier, 'but what can I do?'

'You must talk to them,' said the residents of the fourth floor. 'You must ask them really and truly, to be quiet.'

But then, suddenly, quietness fell.

Stefan helped to stow all Guido Albi's green and tan luggage into the chauffeured car and he was driven away. Before he left, he gave Madame Moutier a handsome tip and apologised for the disturbance he'd caused. He said he was very sad about everything, but the apartment belonged to Claudette now and he wouldn't be coming back.

Madame Moutier looked at the stash of notes she'd been given and counted them and gave 200 francs to Stefan. 'There you are,' she said. 'And we'll have some peace now.'

But Stefan understood that, although no sound came from the fifth floor flat, 'peace' wasn't a word that anyone should be using.

He knew what was really happening to Claudette Albi up there alone. She had been Guido Albi's wife for seventeen years. Jenni Chen was twenty-four and Claudette was forty-five. She was entering a nightmare from which there was no exit.

∞

A YEAR PASSED.

Stefan's drinking became so heavy, Madame Moutier threatened to throw him out if he didn't get a grip on himself. She knew he stole money from her purse when he went on his sprees.

She also knew that whenever the residents saw him reeling home drunk, they were shocked and disgusted and that he was putting her own future in danger.

And she knew something else. Stefan sometimes reverted to doing what he had been forbidden to do as a boy: he sat on the stairs outside the Albis' apartment.

But he didn't care. He wasn't listening to Schubert or Brahms. He was just *waiting* for the day when Claudette would start playing the piano again. He rested his back against the iron banisters. Memories of his childhood came and went. The stairwell grew dark. Sometimes, he fell into a deep sleep.

The winter was unusually cold. Stefan told his mother that he stayed in the bars and cafés to keep warm, but she knew better. She understood now that her livelihood was in jeopardy. Everything she'd worked for – on her own for all these years – was just being pissed away down the toilet.

∾

THEN, ONE ICY MORNING, Claudette Albi appeared at Madame Moutier's door.

She'd wrapped herself in a black mohair shawl and her dark hair was wild.

She asked Madame Moutier if Stefan could come up to her flat. She said she was freezing to death up there because her boiler kept cutting out.

'Oh, I'm sorry,' said Madame Moutier, 'Stefan doesn't work for the gas company any more, Madame Albi. Not since the accident.'

'I know,' said Claudette. 'That's why I need him. I've run out of patience with the gas company. They've been round twice and this morning the boiler's cold again. I want him to sort it out.'

Stefan was still in bed, sleeping off his hangover. He shaved

133

and dressed as quickly as he could and went up the stairs to the fifth floor. He had never been inside the Albis' apartment, never further than their little hallway to deliver flowers or crates of champagne. He took with him his fitter's tool kit, unused for more than a year.

Claudette showed him into her beautiful rooms, which did feel cold, as if no one had been living in them for a long time.

'You see?' she said, 'I can't live up here like this, can I, Stefan?'

'No,' he said. 'You can't.'

She took him to the boiler and he knelt down in front of it and opened its casing. He saw immediately that the pilot light was out and he thought that all he would need to do would be to relight it. But each time he tried to relight it, it extinguished itself and he had to think for a moment to remember the likely reason for this. Then he turned to Claudette, who was crouching beside him. He put his fist in front of his mouth, so that she wouldn't smell the drink on his breath.

'It's the over-ride,' he said. 'This black thing here. It's a safety device. It cuts off the gas if, for any reason, the pilot light goes out. Normally, it can be re-set in order to relight the appliance.'

'Well,' said Claudette, 'that's ridiculous. The gas people already fitted a new one of those black things, but this new one must be faulty too. So what am I to do?'

Stefan turned back to the boiler. He ran a test on the over-ride and found that its trigger was jumping too soon, allowing no gas at all to be fed to the pilot. He said: 'I'm sorry, Madame Albi. The gas company will have to come back. I can't adjust the over-ride. They'll have to put in another new one for you.'

Claudette stood up. She said she would make coffee in her espresso machine for both of them. Then she said: 'Stefan, I'm tired of being cold. While I make the espresso, disconnect the stupid over-ride and get the boiler going.'

∞

HE WAS IN THE APARTMENT with Claudette Albi for about half an hour. When the radiators began to heat up, he checked them for air locks and leaks. In the music room, he saw that the shutters were closed and the grand piano covered with dust sheets.

He drank the strong coffee and Claudette Albi thanked him and pressed into his hand a crumpled fifty franc note, and then he left.

As he went down the stairs, he felt strangely happy, just as if he'd worked some miracle. And, in a small way, he had. What had been missing in those rooms was warmth and this is what his professional expertise had enabled him to supply. He thought, from now on, from this moment, perhaps Claudette Albi will start to play the piano again.

∞

BUT CLAUDETTE ALBI KNEW she would never play the piano again. She knew that a vast, unending silence had settled over her life.

She waited until nightfall. Then, she switched off the boiler and opened the glass casing that covered the gas burner. She extinguished the pilot light.

She lay her head on a cushion as near as she could get to the burner with its pinprick escape holes for the sweet and sickly gas and moved the boiler switch to ON. Dying, she thought, is identical to living: it consists only in breathing.

∞

MADAME MOUTIER WANTED to keep the news of Claudette Albi's death from Stefan. But it couldn't be kept from anyone. For forty-eight hours, the whole building was under siege from the police and the press. Nobody thought to question the Moutiers about the defective state of Madame Albi's boiler.

MONTHS PASSED. Madame Moutier knew how Stefan had admired and revered the Albis and she was afraid this latest catastrophe would pitch him even further down into his spiral of drink and depression.

But this didn't happen. In fact, by the time the warm weather came again, Stefan Moutier seemed, at last, to be coming out of his nightmare.

It was difficult to understand exactly why. He himself wasn't absolutely certain. But he knew that losing Claudette Albi had something to do with it.

It was as if, once both the Albis were gone and he knew that no more Beethoven or Debussy would ever come out of that apartment, Stefan had over-ridden his distant past and with it, the more recent past of his own tragedy. He had left them both behind and was now able to turn his face towards the future. In this future, he told himself, there would one day arrive a different kind of music.

∞

THE
LAST PICNIC

James Hamilton-Paterson

I SUPPOSE IT SEEMS STRANGE NOW – contrived, even obsessive – that after our mother died my father used to take us children each year for a picnic on the same spot. He wasn't a religious man but maybe this ritual had about it as much of the sacramental as he would allow himself, commemorating our last family holiday together.

From a summery backdrop one year suddenly emerged a small man in stained trousers and, despite the heat, a Fair Isle sweater with many holes among its jigsaw patterns. Sitting around our tablecloth spread on the ground, glasses of ginger beer balanced between tufts, we resentfully watched his approach.

'I am Dr Schumann,' this gentleman announced, looking at us in turn. 'I'm so happy you've found my favourite spot.' He extended his hand.

My father, half rising, took it courteously on our behalf, caught in mid-role between the paterfamilias put out by the intrusion into a family occasion and the experienced GP who smells derangement and opts for prudence. 'And I am Dr Sanders. Yes indeed, a lovely spot. Er… we'll have finished with it by and by.'

'Ah, a medical man? I'm afraid I'm only a musician. You may perhaps have heard of me. Schumann? Robert Schumann?'

My sister Caroline and I saw an expression cross our father's face. It was the look when, in the middle of Christmas lunch, the phone rang and called him away to a bedside: noble, martyred, apologetic, and perhaps with the tiniest fraction of relief.

'You can't be *the* Schumann, the composer.' Caroline was the family's pianist. 'He's dead, you know. Yonks ago.' Maybe she caught the fierce glance our father shot at her but at thirteen, my elder by a couple of years, she was not so easily squashed. 'Why did you make everything you wrote so difficult, then?'

Our visitor looked very tenderly at her and said: 'You remind me of my darling Clara.' I could sense my father stir uneasily. 'She was a wonderful pianist, better than I ever became. I wrote nearly everything for her. What, in particular, are you thinking of?'

'Well, how about *Carnaval*? That's awful. I'm supposed to learn some of it this holiday.'

'But that's the very subject of a story I have to tell you,' cried the self-styled composer, leaning forward and plucking up our last sausage roll with a squirrel's agility. 'Listen. You have to imagine I'm nineteen and already embarked on a career as a concert pianist. I was even celebrated enough to have demonstrated Harrods' Steinway collection. I played there an hour each teatime for a week in between engagements. On the last day a lady approached me and said: "Maestro. This weekend we're having a masked ball. You're going to play Schumann for us, I've quite decided. You may name your own fee, but in return you must agree to obey my instructions to the letter. I'm determined you shall come. Dear, divine maestrino that you are – handsome, cheeky thing in private, though, I daresay." She squeezed my hand. "You shall dress as Schumann, of course.

And – Clara awaits you. Such a Clara, too. Dangerously young. Tomorrow you will receive your instructions."

'What could I say? I was myself young, excitable, easily beguiled by mystery. Promptly the next morning a messenger arrived with a sealed envelope and a box containing my costume. "Prepare yourself to play *Carnaval*," the letter said, "even though we already know you play it beautifully. Dress at five; drink nothing; the carriage will call for you at six." I did as instructed. All day I practised music which I'd long known by heart until I could have played all twenty pieces in my sleep and…'

141

'I bet you had a hard time with "Sphinxes",' interrupted Caroline in that slightly-too-casual voice of hers which generally meant a trick question.

Our uninvited guest was not in the least discomfited.

'"Sphinxes", of course, is not written to be played. It's more symbolic: anagrams of the German musical notes A-S-C-H. Asch is the name of a town in Germany where Ernestine, another little friend of mine, lives. The piece can be heard in the heart, my dearest, and you'll never play *Carnaval* well until you can hear my "Sphinxes" in your heart… So anyway, at five I dressed and waited with a strange excitement. At six the doorbell rang and I was ushered into the back seat of a tall Rolls-Royce whose windows were thickly curtained. A man in black handed me a blindfold which he respectfully asked me to put on. Thus, doubly blind, I was driven away. I was thrilled, apprehensive. I felt quite powerless, for in addition to everything else my costume was stiff and unyielding as though it hadn't been worn for a century and was rigid through lack of use. Yet there was no panic in me, for no sooner had we started than the servant in black said in a quiet voice: "I'm instructed

to tell you, sir, that Clara is waiting for you with calmest joy."
And those were the only words he would speak throughout
the journey.

'Eventually,' said the little man through a mouthful of
sausage roll, 'I felt the carriage stop and the door open. "Now
you may take off the blindfold," said my escort. I did so, and
what a spectacle met my eyes! A country house with all its
windows lit up. There were glimpses of a ballroom with people
moving about beneath the twinkle of chandeliers. Liveried
footmen were standing in the *porte-cochère*; one held my door
for me as I climbed out in astonishment. Oh, I can't hope to
convey to you here in broad daylight the magic which seized
me that soft summer dusk, before a great house sparkling with
lights and breathing out its sound of chatter and the distant
strains of music. Have you never felt at the same time happy
and melancholy, not quite knowing what the moment means?
The music I could hear was sad and remote. It spoke of all
things we've never had but still have managed to lose. How can
that be? As I turned my head slightly I was no longer sure it
was coming from the house. It took me a few moments to
recognise my own *Carnaval*, the piece called "Chopin", but
arranged for instruments. In its new disguise I found something missing from the piano original. It said to me: "You may
never leave this place, Robert. Can't you feel its spell? Now
you've been here and heard this music your life has already
changed and your future begins anew." And just for an instant
I shivered.

'In the doorway a lady was standing, waiting for me. She
was dressed as though clasped with blossoms and wore a mask
of petals. "I'm Columbine," she said, and I knew her voice as
that of the woman in Harrods. "Welcome, Maestro," and she

curtseyed slightly. "The night is yours. The house is also yours. And everyone in it is yours – for this one weekend. We are all masked. You alone are yourself, unmasked." "And Clara?" I asked. "How shall I know my Clara?" "How do we any of us know our Claras?" she replied. This was more enigmatic than helpful, I have to admit. But never mind – the excitement of it!

'I was shown into the ballroom and as I entered a footman announced in a loud voice, "Mr Robert Schumann!" I had yet to become a Doctor of Music, you see. At once a hush fell and the whole room turned towards me. And what a company it was! Everyone was in the most fantastic costumes, faces hidden behind masks which came down to just beneath their noses so they could eat and drink and... and kiss. It was very thrilling to me, quite sinister, especially their eyes, a wet glitter behind holes cut in metal and cardboard and cloth. Lady Columbine took me firmly by the wrist, led me over and introduced me to them one by one. "This is Pierrot; this is Harlequin; you really must get to know Estrella." They bowed and curtseyed and I noticed that one or two held my hand longer than was strictly necessary. And all the time I was wondering: Which of them is my Clara? Is it she, with the small extra pressure of those gloved fingers? Or that one? Or that, with almost a child's teeth bared by her smile?

'Lady Columbine clapped her hands. "We shall all go through to the music room and, when our young maestro has collected himself after his long journey and these introductions, he will I hope play for us with his usual magic. From now on, the other world has ceased to exist." And at that moment, happening to glance through the French windows, I saw that the lights in the drive outside had been turned off, that the tall Rolls which had brought me had vanished, that nothing but darkness pressed up against the panes. Footmen now moved from window to window closing the shutters, drawing curtains, sealing the house. Yet all the time, from which room I couldn't tell, I seemed to hear the same melancholy tune I'd heard on my arrival. I never thought my own music could sound so wistful. Did you ever play that, dearest?' the little man broke off to ask my sister, who started as if in a trance. 'Did you ever play "Chopin"?'

'I've learned some Chopin,' said Caroline warily. 'Bits.'

'No, no, my "Chopin" from *Carnaval*.'

'Oh, that one. Yes, that's not too difficult. It's lovely. Really.'

∞

ALL THIS WHILE I had been aware of my father's unease. His silence was eloquent to us, as were his small movements which represented the tension of good manners struggling with anxiety about what this weird fellow would say next. The unbidden guest at our tablecloth had an oddly compelling way of speaking so that my father's reluctance to interrupt was understandable for reasons other than politeness. Even as I stared at the flakes of pastry caught among the patterns of the Fair Isle sweater I almost believed I, too, could hear distant music and see the costumed figures.

'Eventually,' the little man resumed, 'I sat down and played *Carnaval*. I played without music, of course. Two tall candles stood on either side shedding their soft yellow glow. It was a remarkable instrument and I did things that night I'd never done before, found things in my own music I hadn't known were there. As I reached "Chopin" a sigh went around as if at last everyone was hearing what until then had been only half heard, not quite audible. And I knew that none of us there would ever forget it.

'When I'd finished the whole work everyone was all over me, I can tell you. I'm not being immodest. I never bettered that performance and I doubt that anybody ever has. Servants went around with champagne and *bonbonnières* containing little sugared balls which had a positively magical effect on us. Sated with music, we all began to sparkle. I can't remember the dishes I ate, the glasses I drank, not even – I have to say it – the lips I kissed. For how else was I to find my Clara? She was there somewhere, that divine child; I could feel her presence all the time I was playing. The house was full of her elusiveness, mask upon mask upon mask. I pursued her all over it, from one dark bedroom to another, in closet and passageway, in attic and on back staircase. And after each encounter – no! Exquisite, but that wasn't her. A little too old, a fraction too knowing, not completely sincere about the music... *My* music, which after all must have gone straight to her heart.

'Time no longer existed. For all I knew day had long since dawned outside the shuttered windows, midday come and gone, another night fallen. There was nothing in the world but the golden pursuit of masked figures and all the while this faint music. Until finally, in a forgotten servant's room in a disused wing, I came to the end of my search. From behind the door I could hear her voice, a child's voice since she was barely thirteen, singing my haunting melody. I...'

'... wonder if you'd like a cup of tea?' my father broke in, getting to his feet and pulling the Thermos out of the basket. 'And then I suppose we'd better think about a move. The traffic, you know. The Leatherhead bypass especially.' His firm, professional voice and the sound of Bakelite and unscrewing and pouring tore us back to a normality which felt most peculiar. The little man was rocking mutely on his birch stump, red in the face with the agitation of his story. There was a feeling that something awful had been headed off in the nick of time.

'So,' said my father, handing him a mug of tea, 'do you still compose, Dr Schumann?'

'Oh… oh, thank you. Oh yes, yes, I do. The tunes won't let me alone.'

Sympathy must have prompted my sister's surprising intervention. 'I'd like to learn some of your new pieces so long as they're not too difficult,' she said encouragingly. I noticed she was gripping the toe of my father's shoe.

The little man turned on her the most extraordinary, wrenched smile while the tea trickled unheeded from his tilted cup on to his already stained trousers. 'Why, yes,' he cried. 'My dearest one, I've searched for you high and low to give you them. My Clara.'

It was an instant which froze us all. I remember the thick thrill in my stomach when I saw the tears run down the little man's face. This was the moment for my father to interpose decisively; yet again it was my sister who seemed more capable of a reasonable response, as if she were touched rather than frightened by the stranger's pathetic charm.

'I'm afraid my name isn't Clara,' she told him. 'Awfully sorry.'

'Not Clara?' he whispered.

'No. I'm Caroline.'

'Caroline.' He stared at a clump of bracken. 'But it nearly contains her. The anagram, you see. One letter short. So nearly. Always so nearly.' He dried his face with his sweater. 'Never mind. These days it's getting late and you're a dear, sweet child and a pianist as well so I want you to have them.'

∞

HE BEGAN TO WRESTLE in his trousers, tugging at a pocket. An object flew out and landed rattling in the middle of the table-cloth but the man's attention was on the crumpled pages he had found. He smoothed them and we could see music manu-script with notes and staves. 'There,' he said, now on his feet and handing them down to my sister with an archaic bow. I wondered for a moment if he would kiss her hand but he became distracted by the lost object my father was holding out to him. 'Ah, my *bonbonnière*,' he said with a dire wink. 'Thank you, doctor.'

I had recognised it at once as a pillbox: one of those circular off-white affairs made of pleated waxed paper. You don't see them nowadays. My father had given its label a know-ing glance and now said, 'You might perhaps take one, Mr Pinckney?' But something in the little man's mood had broken for he only repeated: 'Never mind, it's getting late,' before muttering, 'It's been charming. Quite like old times,' while hurrying away without a backward glance, head bent, his awful sweater quickly lost among the dapples of the tree trunks.

Nobody said much as we rapidly repacked the picnic things. All I could register was an eleven-year-old's certainty that we would never be coming back to this spot. Other ghosts had taken the place of my mother's. On the way back to the car my father took a short cut across the flank of a wooded hill which suddenly afforded us an unexpected downward view. In the middle distance stood a grim Victorian pile from one of whose outbuildings rose a brick smokestack like that of a steam laun-dry. He paused. 'And that, I fear, is the magical country house.'

Once we were safely back in the car I asked, 'Was he mad?'

'Rather off his chump, I'd say,' came the diagnosis.

'But harmless really,' said Caroline.

'No doubt,' said my father with a fretful smile. 'No doubt.'

The pages the little man had presented to her seemed nowhere to be found and for some time there was nothing tangible to remind us of our haunted picnic. Months later they turned up in the AA book; Caroline must have dropped them into the Wolseley's door pocket. The crotchets and quavers were indecipherable; the crude, aching drawings were not.

All this was long ago, of course, and now our father, too, is dead. Certain of his details are already slipping away. But to this day when Caroline can be persuaded to play *Carnaval* the music at once brings back an intense memory of faces sliding one behind the other – our mother, our father, the little man and his sad fantastic company, all moving in that far-off summer glade with the unease of an inexhaustible longing. Our yearnings, it seems, express us more memorably than do our compromised equanimities. The piece called "Chopin" has a particular effect on Caroline. She once described it as claiming an unfair intimacy, like being made love to in public by a perfect stranger.

∾

CORPORATE
ENTERTAINMENT

Helen Simpson

'B UT YOU LOVE OPERA,' he said. 'Particularly the early stuff. I know you do.'

'Yes,' she said. 'I do.'

'So what's the problem?' he said. 'Try that red thing on now.'

She was standing in her underwear with clothes in piles round her feet, while he lolled on the bed. Since the children and then the loss of her job she had retreated into a shambles of soft leggings and sweatshirts, merely day versions of her pyjamas, except on occasions like now, when, kicking and screaming, she was dragged out for Client Entertainment. Then Christopher showed sudden interest in what she wore, as keen-eyed on the effect of this or that dress as any old-style libertine.

'Front stalls, gala performance,' he persisted. '*Orpheus and Eurydice*. Just right for a wedding anniversary, I'd have thought. Hold your stomach in, Janine. No, it's still no good. Try that black skirt again with the beaded top.'

'It's just about my favourite opera of all,' she panted, hating her reflection in the mirror. 'So fresh and unencumbered and straight to the heart. But.'

'But what,' he said.

'But not with clients,' Janine said reluctantly, as she knew this would enrage him.

'What difference does it make?' he asked. 'They're all

perfectly all right people. You're always on about how you like people.'

When he talked like this, she regarded it as a temporary madness in his life which she would have to put up with, like Pamina walking through the fire with Tamino, and have faith that they would be together again once he was over it.

'Clients aren't friends,' she said.

'They *can* be,' he said. 'You're so narrow-minded. They can become very *good* friends.'

'No,' she mumbled. 'Clients are about money.'

'Oh, wicked Mammon,' he hooted. '*Everything's* about money if you're talking in that ignorant way. Music certainly is. Look at Covent Garden for goodness' sake!'

'Clients are business,' she persisted, 'Not pleasure.'

'Client entertainment is *all about* pleasure,' he snarled. 'Good tickets, champagne, the works. You used to be more generous-spirited.'

'You can't get drunk with clients,' she said.

'You certainly can,' said Christopher. 'I do.'

'True,' she conceded. 'But you couldn't ever be really rude or insulting to clients.'

'You won't keep many friends that way either.'

'You don't make friends for their usefulness,' she said. 'There can't be strings attached.'

'Why not?' he said. 'Mutually beneficial relationships, that's the way the world works. *Special* relationships; hadn't you heard? Symbiotic's the word. Hadn't you *noticed*?'

'Is that why you married me?' she asked. 'Because of what I could do for you.

'Obviously not,' he said with some truculence.

There was silence. He looked her straight in the eye.

'No,' he said.

'Good,' she said, and went and lay beside him on the bed.

'Your smell,' she said at last, her face in his shoulder. 'That's how I know it's still you.'

∞

'MUSIC! ME, I'm mad for it,' said Nigel Perkins from Littleboy and Pringle. 'All sorts. Depends on my mood. Verdi when I'm down. Which isn't often. A bit of Bowie. Some Cajun. Eine Kleine Nacht music. It's like food really, isn't it. Like Shakespeare said.'

Janine nodded and smiled.

'It's what you're feeling like at the time,' he continued. 'I usually listen in the car to be honest, or on the Walkman. Like most of us. So this'll be a novelty.'

'Do you know the story?' asked Janine.

'No,' he said. 'I guess I'll pick it up as I go along.'

'Um, but they're singing in French,' said Janine. 'It's the Berlioz version. Orpheus was a singer whose music charmed the wild beasts. Then his wife Eurydice died suddenly. He went down to the underworld looking for her…'

'Janice, Janice,' he said. 'It's OK! I get the drift.'

'Sorry,' said Janine.

'I think it ruins these things if you analyse them,' he said, looking round for more champagne. 'All that chatterchatter-chatter.'

'Mmm,' went Janine.

'Ah, here's my wife. Penny! This is Christopher's wife, Janice.'

'Hi,' said Penny. 'Horrific journey, darling. Mega hold-up at Sevenoaks. Now, who's this Gluck fellow?'

'Born in Bohemia, studied in Italy,' said Janine before she could stop herself. 'Visited London, made friends with Handel, wrote an opera celebrating the Battle of Culloden, which flopped. Then he went to Vienna and...'

'Now then Janice!' said Nigel Perkins playfully. 'Chatter-chatterchatter.'

'The mummies on the bus go chatterchatterchatter,' sang Penny brightly.

'What?' said her husband.

'It's a nursery school song,' muttered Janine. 'Mine sing it too. The daddies on the bus go rustlerustlerustle. Their news-papers, you see.'

'Ladies and gentlemen, the performance is about to begin,' announced a waiter, shimmying up to their group and holding out a tray for empty glasses.

'Any idea how long it is to half-time?' enquired Nigel Perkins.

'I'm not quite sure, sir, but I believe it's a very short opera.'

'That's good,' said Penny as they made their way to the audi-torium. 'Time to enjoy the meal in the interval that way. Not like in *Pelleas and Melisande*.'

'No, that was terrible!' agreed her husband. 'Massive long affair that was and only two fifteen-minute breaks.'

'Awful,' said Penny, shaking her head. 'Bolting down Coronation Chicken in the first interval, if you could *call* it an interval, then not-very-nice blueberry cheesecake in the second one and no time to finish your coffee. This is *much* nicer,' she said, turning to Janine with a gracious smile.

IN THE DARK, listening to the music, Janine lifted away from the world of people and things. She forgot about the shadowy pin-stripes each side of her and concentrated on the stage, where mourners like moving white statues tossed flowers on Eurydice's tomb. The bereaved husband Orpheus lay pole-axed by grief while the chorus of mourners sang their beautiful lament. 'Eurydice!' cried Orpheus, and she felt the frisson in her flesh. 'Eurydice!' he cried again, interrupting the mourners, and she sighed. Then for a third time he cried out 'Eurydice!' and this time she jumped, for Nigel Perkins was whispering in her left ear.

'That's cheerful,' he was hissing. 'Kicking off with a funeral.'

On stage the spirit of Hymen extinguished his torch to show marriage sundered by death, and the chorus sang:

L'amoureuse tourterelle   155
Toujours tendre, toujours fidèle
Ainsi soupire et meurt de douleur.

Again Janine felt the unwelcome warmth of Nigel Perkins's breath in her ear.

'I said, *look*, they've got surtitles,' he whispered noisily. 'You needn't have worried about me after all.'

Janine forced herself to nod and smile.

'Nice of you, though,' he added, huskily.

At this point someone in the row behind shushed him and he settled back into his seat and shut up.

Was it marriage itself which had died, then, she wondered, returning to the other world; was it this ideal of turtle doves and fidelity, of the long haul flight without betrayal which had proved unworkable? Orpheus sang with mounting grief, urgent and controlled. It was coming back to her now, the particular quality of distress in this opera, where from the start something terrible has happened; something irreversible. And that's just like death, she thought. The line has been crossed and everything has changed.

The music had stolen up on her like hot water flooding over her skin. She remembered that morning in the half-hour before waking, how a procession had trooped through her mind of all the people she had loved who were now dead. Last time Christopher had come home drunk from a client reception, she had wondered aloud whether he would notice if she died, and he had said how he bet she would *like* him dead then she would have no more pain or trouble. She stifled a groan.

Now Amor was informing Orpheus in cheery silvered tones that the Gods had taken pity on him and would allow him down into the infernal regions to fetch Eurydice back to life, on one condition. He must not look at her while in the precincts of the dead, nor tell her why not.

Soumis au silence

Contrains ton désir

Fais-toi violence

sang Amor, and above the stage the surtitles slid past: In obedient silence Hold your longing in check Go against your every instinct. The words flew at her and landed in her like arrows. Wait in silence, yes, that was what was required of her, with the traditional carrot that love would be rewarded. But, she thought wrathfully, unlike in operas, we grow old while waiting in silence.

Orpheus was facing the Furies now, their rancorous music with booms and blaring from the horns, their flashing strings and fierce runs in octaves. He waited, then pleaded with the help of harp and flute to be allowed down to the kingdom of the dead. Again and again the Furies refused him, but at last his entreaties softened their hearts and they let him go. If only, thought Janine. When she said, 'I'm miserable,' to Christopher, *he* said, 'No you're not.' When she raged at him like one of the Furies, he said, 'I love you.' Unfair. Unanswerable.

∞

BACK IN THE HOSPITALITY ROOM at the interval, Christopher was all tenderness and attention, hovering dotingly over Dominic Pilling of Schnell-Darwittersbank and hanging on Dominic Pilling's wife's every word.

'London's getting terribly crowded, isn't it,' said the wife. 'Too many people. I'm afraid I'm a country girl at heart.'

'You love gardening,' Christopher suggested fondly.

'Oh yes. Except I get dreadful hay fever,' she said.

'So we have to get someone in to do it,' laughed Dominic.   157

'Because Dominic's not around enough at weekends to guarantee keeping it down,' she said.

'I have better things to do with my leisure time than cut the grass.'

'Like work,' she said nastily.

Janine caught Christopher's eye and looked away again. We'll be like them in five years' time, she thought, if we carry on like this; it's what you do every day that changes you.

'Ah, leisure,' said Christopher hastily. 'That precious commodity. We're just in the process of booking ourselves a holiday, aren't we darling. Where did you go last time?'

'Club Med,' said Dominic Pilling with enthusiasm. 'Brilliant. The actual country you're in is irrelevant. They're all organised to the same very high standards so it hardly matters.'

'You don't have to lift a finger,' cooed Caroline. 'The children are taken care of. You never see them! They adore it.'

'The main thing is to recharge the batteries,' declared Dominic.

'Are you enjoying the opera?' asked Janine.

'Oh it's super,' said Caroline. 'And not too *long* either.'

SITTING IN THE DARK again Janine realised that they had not been out on their own together that year. The music of Elysium came creeping in through her ears, slow, sublime, holding and catching her breath until she sighed deeply and shifted in her seat. He had no time for her. This must be what music was for, she thought, so while on the outside you moderated and rationalised and subdued, in your secret self you were allowed to live with an intensity not otherwise sanctioned. He was never there. Now the orchestral music became more complex, an oboe melody with rippling triplet accompaniment from the strings, braided like the surface of a fast-flowing river or like the patterned weavings of thought and feeling, trouble and desire.

158

Eurydice was pleading with her husband to take her in his arms. She sang her hurt in soft slow soaring phrases and descents. Why was he ignoring her? Was she no longer beautiful to him?

Janine felt a hot prickling sensation behind her face, like walking into a rosebush. Almost the worst thing was being frozen into these corny, passive and wifely attitudes of grief and betrayal. The ravishingly sweet quarrel of their voices blended and untangled, pulling air down into her lungs, making her sigh helplessly.

Eurydice sang, 'Dear husband, I can hardly breathe for sorrow.' Orpheus was protesting his devotion and at the same time crushing her with his indifference. Then at last he cracked. He turned to look back at her. She died instantly. It was the least bombastic of operatic deaths, and the most comfortless. He had misjudged and this time she was lost forever.

As he began his famous aria, 'J'ai perdu mon Eurydice', Janine realised that tears were streaming down her face. For pity's sake, she thought, not here, and tried to wipe them away